Path of the
DRAGON

ASHLEIGH D.J. CUTLER

Crystal Prism Publications
Ohio, United States of America
www.ashleighdjcutler.weebly.com ~ ashwolf-forever.deviantart.com

First Edition 2017

Cutler, Ashleigh, 1985 –

Path of the Dragon by Ashleigh D. J. Cutler – 1st ed.

Front Cover Art by yvonrz
SelfPubBookCovers.com/yvonrz

Publishing Logo Pawprint by Achiha-Azteca
achiha-azteca.deviantart.com

The title is set in Black Chancery and Broken Glass.
The body text is set in Times New Roman and Garamond.

Edited by Cassandra Mehlenbacher and Kirstin van Dyke

ISBN-13: 9780998465906 (Crystal Prism Publications)
ISBN-10: 0998465909

TO THE REAL-LIFE "FREAK SHOW"

I have some of the best friends online I could ask for. They've dried my tears, been a shoulder to lean on, and in general been my biggest support system outside my family. Without them, I might not be here at all. I won't name names because I know I'd miss someone somehow. Just know I love you guys, and thanks for being my friends.

ACKNOWLEDGMENTS

I want to thank the kind, generous people who basically let me borrow their characters to be my supporting cast, both in *Mask of the Dragon*, and this time around too. Once again, no naming names, but you know who you are and you know I couldn't have done this without you.

PROLOGUE

"You can't tell me you actually agree with the stuff Preacher Davidson says," Abby said as she drove home from her grandmother's. She glanced at Marlon in the passenger seat. "So why are you still going?"

"You don't either," he said. He kept rubbing at his pocket to check he hadn't dropped his wallet or something, she assumed. "I promised. A deal's a deal."

"Mars-Bars." She sighed. "You don't make deals with God."

"It's working out so far."

"How did you make a deal with Someone you don't believe in anyway?"

"Desperation," Dominic replied. The Golden Retriever-sized, black-and-white dragon, invisible to all but her, lay stretched out across the back seat. "You'd be surprised what you'll bargain with if it's your only hope."

"Never said I don't believe there's..." Marlon shifted and scratched at the back of his neck. "I mean, maybe there is Something there. Someone. Whoever it is kept Their end, so I'm keeping mine. Besides, it's just one more year, right? Then we can tell Davidson good-bye."

They came to a stoplight and she turned to look at him. "I appreciate the company, don't get me wrong. But we both shouldn't have to suffer." She smiled. "I know you said if I changed churches, you'd follow. But when I go back to Mass, I'll be fine."

"It's no big deal, Abs." He took hold of her old cross, which he still wore alongside the pendant bearing his family's crest. He slid it back and forth on the chain. "If I ever wanna quit you'll be the first to know, OK?"

"You might as well drop it." Dominic laid his head on his paws, tail dangling off the seat. "He's a Samson. They don't break promises."

Abby just shook her head. She pulled into the parking space outside her great-aunt's apartment. She got out and unlocked the back door to the 1985 Monte Carlo she'd inherited from her parents. *There's no reason he should...* She couldn't think of the words.

"Do what you've had to all these years?" The Dragon finished for her. He slipped past her as she grabbed the bag with her birthday gifts. She slammed the car door. "Misery loves company."

That's pretty much what I just said. Abby hung the bag on her arm, then shifted to get to the apartment key, eager to get out of the July heat. Before she could unlock the door, Marlon laid his hand on her arm. She turned and met his nervous gaze.

"Abs?" He reached into his pocket and pulled out a small circular charm. "Um, I..." He reached out and, after missing the link twice, clipped it to her bracelet right beside the dragonfly. "Here."

Abby raised her wrist to get a look at the charm. It took her only a moment to recognize his family's crest. She kept her eyes on the charm as her face heated up. "Marlon... uh..."

"It's no big deal," he said quickly. "Just... you're family, Abs. And... well." He scratched at his neck and looked at her sheepishly. "I was thinking... uh... canwegosteadynowplease?"

It took Abby a moment to make sense of what he said before her jaw dropped. She felt her mouth move, but no sound would come out. *Steady? Did he really just say that?* Whenever she'd considered their becoming official, she thought it would come sometime after high school graduation.

"Do not be dense, Abigail," Aeneas' resigned voice echoed in her ears. "It does not suit you."

"That's my line," complained Dominic. The Dragon nudged her side with his shoulder. "Are you going to answer the boy, or what?"

Aunt Gladys won't... Then again, Gladys constantly praised how well "that boy" was doing "despite his troubled home life." The fact Marlon was at her side every Sunday, silent and his eyes locked on the Preacher as if his life depended on it, went a long way toward changing minds. Abby was one of the few who was aware his piety was as much a show as her own.

"What's the worst that could happen?" Marlon fidgeted then took a deep breath. "If... ifwe'rebetterasfriendsthencoolwecallitoff." He started babbling too fast for her to follow.

"The boy is going to bite his tongue off at this rate." Dominic shook his head. "What's the problem? It's not like he's down on one knee, after all." He rolled his eyes. "And even if he was, he wouldn't be as cheesy as your friend the rat. St. Valentine's of all days."

I sure hope that isn't what prompted this. Drew and Melissa had been married within five months of their February engagement at the insistence of his parents. Swallowing hard, Abby reached out and took Marlon's hand then smiled. She took a deep breath. "Yes."

Marlon froze in place. "Yes?" He grinned like Christmas had come early. "Really?"

Abby couldn't help but laugh. She nodded. "Marlon, seriously. It's been unspoken for almost a year." *And I was perfectly fine with that.* They loved each other, and both knew it. It didn't need to be shouted from the rooftops. "And obvious enough to get teased for."

"Grandpa's a dork sometimes." Marlon rolled his eyes, relief written all over his face. "See ya tomorrow, Abs." He squeezed her hand then headed to his family's apartment next door. "Thank you."

"See ya, Mars-Bars." Abby unlocked the door, then went straight to her room.

At least Aunt Gladys and Mrs. Davidson aren't back yet. She set her gifts on her desk and pulled the chair out. The new charm caught the light and she smiled. She started to sit down then stumbled backwards when she met no resistance, slamming into the floor. A hiss escaped her as she rubbed her hip. She turned and glared at the chair. "I know I'm not that ..." Familiar laughter rang out and she scrambled to her feet, backing up until she hit the wall. "No."

Dominic's low growl echoed in her ears. "You -"

"Hey kids," said Bjarte as he appeared beside her bedroom door. Abby's personal demon still wore the form of a blue-eyed man with spiked blond hair, dressed in black. His grin was just as chilling as she remembered. "Miss me?"

Aeneas materialized beside her and glared. "Child's pranks?" Abby's guardian moved to her side, his stance not unlike a mother wolf over her pups. "Is there any low you will not sink to?"

"Why so surprised, Abs?" Bjarte folded his arms and leaned against the far wall. "You seriously didn't think ya got rid of me that easily? Told ya you aren't a priest and even if you were, you're stuck with me..." His grin widened as he smirked at Aeneas. "Can't have one without the other."

"Go away," said Abby, ashamed to hear her voice tremble. She reached up and stroked the cross Marlon had given her for Christmas, trying to tell herself the chill she felt was due to the air conditioning. "You aren't welcome here."

"Don't matter," said the demon. "I'm assigned to ya, remember? Gonna have to learn to deal." His eyes went to her hand on the

cross. "Still, seems you'd rather laugh with the sinners than cry with the saints, Ginny."

"Her name is Abigail," snapped Dominic as he put himself between them. "Even a child remembers the names of its toys."

"I ain't a child, and she ain't either." Bjarte gave Aeneas a dirty look. "Seriously Annie, knock off the puppet show."

Abby took a shaky step forward. She took comfort in the illusion of burying her hand into Dominic's golden mane. Just because it was all in her head didn't make it less comforting. She drew a deep breath. "I've... I've got this, Grandpa Nick." She narrowed her eyes. It somehow felt good to reveal the true identity of The Dragon "Dominic" to her demon. "Sorry to disappoint, but there's no mask here for you to wear anymore. Now, maybe I can't get rid of you, but that doesn't mean I'm listening. So scat!"

Bjarte stared at The Dragon, a stunned expression on his face.

Dominic laughed. "What's the matter, deceiver? You look like you've seen a ghost."

"That's not fair!" Bjarte's voice rose in fury. "It's always been one player per team. He can't be here playin' sidekick!"

The Dragon shrugged. "Take it up with your 'boss' if you don't like it. You don't have to take our word for it."

"Maybe I will!" Bjarte stomped his foot, turned on his heel and vanished.

"Might not be a child," Dominic noted, snorting. "But he sure acts like one."

Shaking, Abby slid down to her knees and pressed her hands to the floor. "He's back. Oh... what am I going to do?"

"Ignore him like the tantruming child he is," said Aeneas. He rested a reassuring hand on her shoulder. "Your fate is yours to shape."

Easier said than done, she thought, digging her fingers into the carpet.

CHAPTER 1

Abby reread, for the third time, the official-looking handwritten letter she had found beside her breakfast plate. Face burning, she met her great-aunt Gladys' smug gaze. "Is this some kind of joke?"

"I'm afraid not, Abigail. As you pointed out, you are eighteen years old and can make your own choices." The older woman sipped her tea. "And I refuse to have a heretic in my home. I cannot support you returning to that house of sin." She tsked. "I so hoped I had raised you better."

"Heretic, my ass!" shouted Dominic. The Dragon crouched on the floor, looking ready to spring. "Guess it was stupid to expect understanding and tolerance from the old bat, but still she waited this long to pull this stunt?"

Abby started shaking, torn between fury and fear. *Why am I surprised?* She had announced her intentions to return to the Catholic faith on her birthday a month prior, hoping her great-aunt would respect her decision. At the time, Gladys had only asked if she had thought it through. Abby had assured her that she had, and as a legal adult the choice was her own. Gladys had simply nodded. Nothing more had been said on the subject, even when she and Marlon had started attending mass rather than Preacher Davidson's services. And now this. *What am I going to do?*

"You'd best be getting along, dear." Gladys looked at the clock on the wall. "You'll be late for school. I hope that still matters to you."

Abby pushed out of her chair with a screech, pocketing the letter. She picked up the backpack at her feet and swung it over her shoulders. Her gaze darted to her untouched plate, all appetite gone. Locking eyes with Gladys, Abby pulled her crucifix out from under her top to rest in plain sight. "Good day, Aunt Gladys." She turned on her heel and stormed out the front door before her temper could get the better of her.

At lunch, Abby sat her tray down on the cafeteria table across from Marlon's sister. She all but plopped into the chair he pulled out for her. "Hey, Felice."

"Hey." Felice looked up from her tray and narrowed her eyes. "What's up?"

"The sky?" She fought to open her milk with shaking hands. *I don't even know how to... what do I say? "Aunt Gladys gave me forty-eight hours to get out 'cause I'm Catholic"?*

Unfortunately, her boyfriend wasn't having it. "Abs, spill. What's eating you?" Marlon asked, his expression concerned as he took his place beside her, arms folded in front of his tray.

"Nothing," she replied, fighting to keep her voice steady. She picked up the apple on her tray and rolled it in her hands. "I'm at the top of the food chain."

"Might as well tell them," said Dominic, curling up behind her. "You know Little Wasp won't let it rest. Since you two made it official he's been as much a love-sick fool as his grandfather."

Aeneas interjected. "You also do not need him panicking again." Unlike The Dragon, Aeneas tended to keep out of sight. Likely because Abby was often tempted to slap him upside the head.

Mind your own business, she mentally snapped. She ignored Dominic's growl and took a bite of her apple, her chewing temporarily drowning out their voices and buying her time.

Melissa flopped into her chair with a sigh. She dropped her lunch bag on the table and her backpack to the floor. "Drew lucked out. I swear the course load this year is crazy." She pulled her thermos out of the bag and took a drink. "Of course, that bible college place seems nuttier than a bag of trail mix."

"Given who runs it? That's not surprising" Abby took another bite of her apple and swallowed it whole. "Why are you complaining about the classes? You could be home right now." She glanced at the two rings shining on her friend's left hand and smirked. *"Mrs. Davidson."*

Melissa flushed and busied herself with getting out her lunch. "I'm not Mrs. Davidson," she muttered, "my mother-in-law is."

"Is the honeymoon over then?" asked Felice innocently, laughing when their friend's face turned as red as Abby's apple.

"So what's up with you all?" said Melissa, obviously trying to change the subject. She unwrapped her sandwich and took a bite.

"Abs was about to tell us what's bothering her," replied Marlon, narrowing his eyes. He crossed his legs and arms, then shoved his chair half-backwards, rocking it to an angle. "Weren't you?"

"Sit your chair back down, Mars-Bars, before you crack your skull open."

"There is no need to take your anger out on him, Abigail," came Aeneas' scolding tone.

No one asked you, Jiminy Cricket. Abby forced her voice to a softer tone. "Your pizza's getting cold. I don't wanna hear your stomach growling because you didn't eat your lunch."

Marlon let his chair drop back down to the floor with a bang. He reached out, picked up the slice of pizza off his tray, took a deliberate bite and swallowed. "Your food's getting cold too, you know. Abs, come on… this is me you're talkin' to." He flashed a grin then hit her with the puppy eyes. "Please?"

Any other time, that would have made her day. Right then, though…. "Fine." Abby jerked the letter from her pocket and slid it across the table to him. "That's what's wrong. Happy now?" She picked up her slice and took a huge bite in an effort to control her fury. *It's not Marlon's fault I have no idea what I'm going to do.* She wanted to cry. She swallowed hard and reached for her drink with every intention to keep her mouth full until she got control of her herself.

Marlon read the letter, his expression growing darker and darker with every second.

"You done it now," said Dominic, folding his ears. "You done kicked the Wasp nest."

I believe Aunt Gladys threw this rock, Dommy. Abby took another bite of her pizza. She chewed carefully, watching her boyfriend warily. *Three… two… one.*

"THAT BITCH!" Marlon's outburst startled not just Melissa and Felice, but their neighbors at the next two tables. He stood up, shoving his chair backwards onto the floor. "THAT –"

"Marlon!" said Felice firmly, reaching out and grabbing her brother's arm. "Sit back down," she hissed, "you're making a scene. And for the swear jar, that'll be one –" She carefully pulled the letter out of his hand and started reading, her mouth gaping. "Never mind. This one's on the house. How dare she!"

"She who? What are you –?" Felice handed Melissa the letter and her eyes darted across the page. Melissa carefully set it on the table, reached into a pocket, and handed Felice a five dollar bill before adding her own colorful opinion to the mix. "Drew's gonna flip," she added, "I don't think even my preacher father-in-law would go *that* far."

"Sit back down, Mars-Bars, please." Abby reached out and touched his arm, drawing his attention to her. Whatever he saw in her face made him oblige. Once he was seated, she laid her hand over his.

"Don't worry, Abs. We'll figure out something."

"I seem to remember an offer to move in with you all if she ever did this," said Abby, trying to joke but she heard her voice crack.

"Still stands," said Marlon firmly, intertwining his fingers with hers. "We got this. Hakuna Matata."

"Yeah," Abby said, trying to sound more confident than she felt. She took the letter back with a halfhearted laugh. "No worries."

"OK, we'll deal with this after school." Felice looked over at her brother, then pulled her locket into view. Abby knew it contained the same crest as Marlon's pendant and the charm he had given her. "We got your back, Abby."

"They aren't the only ones." Aeneas and Dominic's words echoed in her head in stereo.

"I know," she answered not only Felice, but her guardians as well.

CHAPTER 2

After school, Drew got out of his car and walked to meet them. "OK, who died? You all look like you belong at a funeral."

"Don't be so dramatic," said Melissa. "Gladys kicked Abby to curb 'cause she's gone Catholic. Gave her an eviction notice this morning. She's got two days to get out."

Drew's face contorted into wide-eyed shock. "She did what?" He looked from his wife and Abby to the Samson twins and back again. "I'll talk to my father. That's... it's unbecoming of a Child of God." He gagged and shook his head. "I am gonna be glad when I graduate. Talking like this is so... I feel like an idiot."

"You sound like one, too." Marlon's smirk matched his teasing tone.

Abby elbowed him in the side before turning to Drew. "Drew, you don't have to do that. I doubt ... sorry but I don't see your father taking my side here."

"Still doing it." Drew opened the door for Melissa, then walked around the car to get behind the wheel once she was safely inside. "We'll see what comes." He pulled out of the parking lot and drove away.

"I don't know how Mel puts up with him." Felice sighed. 'I need to get to work." She got into the car the Samson siblings shared. "Catch you two later."

Once Felice was out of sight, Abby took Marlon's hand in hers and they started walking home. *The Samsons are already crowded, so that's*

11

out. I know there's extended-stay hotels, Abby thought. She racked her brain for the information she'd gathered over the years when she'd plotted her escape. She tightened her grip on her backpack strap as she walked alongside Marlon. *But that won't get my furniture out. Apartments don't rent on such short notice, and even if they did, I couldn't afford it.*

Once she turned eighteen, Abby had gained complete control of what she thought of as her trust fund, and seeing the numbers had been a rude awakening. She'd always known her parents hadn't been rich, but she had assumed there would be more than that left. And since the car she'd inherited from her parents was best described as a gas guzzler, she drove only when she absolutely had to. *I sound like a used car salesman's pitch. "Only driven by a little old lady to church and the grocery store."* She let out a sigh as they rounded the corner to their apartment building. *The next few hours are going to be fun.*

Dominic's smug tone caught her attention. "I think in more ways than one." His ears twitched as they got closer to "home".

What are you talking about? Then the heated argument reached her ears as well. *Oh, crap!* Her eyes followed the voices to find Gladys almost toe-to-toe with Marlon's grandfather Bryan. Marlon's father stood nearby.

"You are not setting foot in my apartment, you wolf in sheep's clothing!" Gladys' clenched hands would have betrayed her fury if her loud voice hadn't already. "Your rock star status means nothing to me. Get out before I call the police!"

"Listen here, you -"

"Dad, let me handle this." Marlon's father Wendel stepped between them. Wendel nudged Bryan back with his shoulder. "Mrs. Lynde, we are simply abiding by the notice you served your niece this morning." Wendel's tone was the complete opposite of Gladys'. "You gave her forty-eight hours to have her property off yours." He jerked a thumb at the U-haul truck behind him. "If you will kindly step aside and allow us to -"

"You aren't touching her things! You'd pawn it soon as look at it! And just how do you know what I served my niece?"

Abby looked at Marlon suspiciously. "Mars-Bars... what did you do?"

"Called Dad when I went to the restroom. Figured he'd know what to do." Marlon's smirk almost made her laugh. "Looks like he did."

Abby sighed and let go of Marlon's hand to close the distance between her and her aunt. "He knows because my *boyfriend* asked what was bothering me at school and called him, Aunt Gladys." She turned and smiled at Wendel. "Evening, Mr. Samson. Bryan."

"I see." Gladys' face was redder than Abby had ever seen it, she crossed her arms in front of her chest as if to keep herself from putting them around one of their necks. "Well! He still isn't setting foot in *my* apartment. I refuse!"

Wendel drew a folded paper from his pocket and shoved it into her hand. "This says we are." He turned and picked up a stack of folded boxes and a roll of packing tape, then pushed past Gladys to get inside. "Come on, Dad. Abby, you'll have to show us where your room is."

Abby scrambled after the Samson men with Marlon on her heels. She flinched as Gladys yelled out once more that if they didn't get out of her home she was calling the law. "Mr. Samson, I'm pretty sure she means it." She moved ahead of them and led them into her room.

"Let her," said Wendel. He put one of the boxes together and tossed it to the floor. "She started this with her 'notice'. I just handed her mine that we're here abiding by hers." He kicked the box over to his son before starting on another. "Any cop that shows will just laugh. You two get the small stuff packed up." The next boxed THUNKED to the floor. "We'll get the heavy crap." He heaved up one end of her trunk. Bryan quickly took the other end and the two were out the door.

Abby blinked. "Maybe you better clear the desk. I'll get the dresser." She rushed to transfer her carefully-folded clothes to the box beside her.

"There anything in here that belongs to the old bat?" Marlon emptied out her desk drawers, cleared off the top, then dragged the box over to her nightstand to toss its contents in, too.

"Not that I know of. The furniture was my grandparents'. Anything she 'bought' me came out of the fund my parents' left behind, and Grandma added onto that." Abby folded the box shut, taped it, and put another together. She sat it beside her closet then jumped as shouted swearing came from the living room. *That sounds like… but it can't be…* She spun and tore down the hallway to the living room. Her jaw dropped. *"Grandma?"*

Gail Whelan stood in a pale summer dress and slip-on shoes, her short gray hair neatly combed. She stood a foot from her sister Gladys, her hands clenched into fists. "I told you twelve years ago and I'm telling you now: you take one more thing from that girl and I will see your pristine reputation *destroyed!* Don't you think for one second I don't still know people in this neighborhood. Now, Wasp and his son are going to oblige *your* request and you are going to shut up about it, or so help me, Gladys, I will knock you into next Sunday and you can hear the sermon early."

"That's my lady," said Dominic, chuckling to himself.

How did she get here? Grandma doesn't drive anymore…

"Hi Grandma," said Marlon, smiling. "Fancy seeing you here."

"Ask a foolish question," replied Aeneas. "And…"

Get a stupid answer. Abby followed Marlon's gaze to find a smug Vera leaning against the doorjamb. "Hello, Mrs. Samson. What brings you and my grandma here?"

"Likely the fact your grandmother can keep this fiasco from being blown any further out of proportion," answered Aeneas the guardian.

I didn't ask you! Abby fought back the urge to rub her temples. *OK, maybe I did but I figured that already, thank you!*

"Hello, dears," Vera said. "Gail and I were just in the neighborhood. We had thought we'd take you two to dinner…" Vera eyed Gladys with disgust. "It appears that will have to be postponed."

Abby sighed and nodded. "Come on, Mars-Bars. We better finish packing." *The sooner I get out of here the better.*

"Amen to that," said Dominic. He laughed at his widow's voice as she soundly put her younger sister in her place.

CHAPTER 3

Abby followed the truck to a place a few minutes from the apartment complex. Marlon rode in the seat beside her and a couple boxes were tossed in the back. It was disturbing how much difference that short distance made. They drove through the oil-stained parking lot of an old plaza only to stop in front of a battered two-story building with a faded sign that read "Moon Shine Down Bar". She looked around from the safety of her car, getting more nervous by the second.

Bars covered the windows and door of the market next door. Some of the shops clearly needed a fresh coat of paint, though not as badly as the bar itself did. One bright spot of white by the door made her wonder if it'd been hit with graffiti. A yellow neon sign in the window, flashing halfheartedly, warned that staff weren't responsible if patrons crossed the line.

The area was everything she'd been warned to avoid most of her life, and she couldn't stop the tremor of fear that went down her spine. She found herself toying with the charm Marlon had given her, rubbing the small circle between her thumb and forefinger.

"It's OK, Abs," said Marlon, gently brushing a stray hair behind her ear. "Grandpa grew up here. You'll be safe. If you weren't, I'd be on the couch at home and you'd be in my bed."

"I'm sure Kenny and Isaac would appreciate that." Abby looked at Marlon. His younger brothers liked her well enough, but that wasn't likely to translate into happily sharing their space. "You ever think your apartment is way too small for your family?"

Marlon looked sheepish, then opened his door before coming around the car to open hers. "Let's get inside before the mosquitoes eat us alive."

They joined Bryan at the bar's front entrance and waited as he flipped through his key ring. In a matter of minutes he reached one that looked as old as the building itself, and unlocked the door. They stepped inside and shut the door behind them.

Abby's first impression was that the place reeked of alcohol and other scents she couldn't place. Her second was that the scuffed up, uneven floor must have been slammed one too many times. *How many fights has this place seen?*

In the dim light, she could just see a stocky older man behind the bar, sweeping the floor in time with a "golden oldies" station playing on a beat-up radio behind him.

"We're closed. If you're here to rob me I don't keep cash in the —" he said as he turned around, saw them and sighed. "Oh, it's just you, Wasp. Expected you and the boys an hour ago."

Bryan crossed the distance and wrapped the old man in a bear hug that was hastily returned by the shorter man before he stepped out of the embrace. "Woulda been here on time but the bitch just had to show her ass."

Sam snapped his fingers and pointed to a mason jar on the counter that looked almost as old as the bar itself. "Two dollars, now. I ain't hearin' about lettin' you cuss in front of me again."

"Swear you fund this place on that thing," Bryan grumbled but pulled out his wallet anyway. He dug a five out of it and dropped it into the jar. "Keep the change, I'll use it up before long."

Marlon gently took Abby's hand and guided her over to the bar, pushing her sleeve back and her charm bracelet into view as he did so. "Sam, I'd like to introduce you to my girlfriend, Abigail Palmer." The smug look on his face made her bite her cheek. "Abs, this is

Sam. He's... pretty much Grandpa's dad. He's run this place since before we were born."

"No 'pretty much' to it," said Bryan, shoving his hands into his pockets. "This guy's one of the reasons I didn't end up dead in alley somewhere."

"Quit makin' me feel old, boy." Sam rolled his eyes and wiped his hands on the bar rag before meeting Abby's gaze. "Heard you got kicked to the curb by your aunt." He snorted. "The crazy loon that hangs around that preacher that Queenie can't stand. Surprised ya made it out physically in one piece. Looks like we got another stray to add to the collection."

Bryan pinched his nose. "V'll love hearin' ya still call her queenie."

Sam shrugged. "She's the one that dresses up as the evil queen for Halloween, and the persona sticks forever."

"What does that make you then?" Abby asked Bryan, amused by the banter.

"Her knight," Sam answered for Bryan, snorting. "Boy, makes quite the picture... and 'bout takes my head off every time it comes up."

"Some things never change," Dominic said, coming to sit beside Abby. He looked around the bar and shook his head, then eyed Bryan and Sam. "Like these two clowns. Someone gonna explain what's going on here or what?"

Abby repeated Dominic's last question aloud. All she had gotten from Marlon on the way over was they had worked out a place for her to stay.

"You're takin' the bumbler's old job," Sam replied, jerking a thumb at Bryan. "And his old room. Rules are simple: You don't touch the booze, and you don't take crap off the customers. They give you any trouble, ya remind 'em we got the right to refuse service.

They don't take the hint, call me over. Other than that, you're on your own."

"How reassuring."

"I'm sure if anything went down, Wasp or Little Wasp would deal with it in a heartbeat."

Abby fought the urge to roll her eyes at her guardians' commentary. *It's a good thing I'm the only one that can hear you.* Instead, she dropped a curtsy. "Thank you, sir." She looked up at Bryan and Marlon. "Thank all of you."

Sam snapped his fingers at Bryan and pointed toward the back of the bar. "Get out there and help your son get her stuff indoors before this gets mushy, will ya?"

"Sure thing, Sam." Bryan clasped his hand onto the old man's shoulder before leading them out the back door.

CHAPTER 4

Abby followed Marlon and Bryan into the alley around back where Wendel had parked the moving truck. They each grabbed a box and walked up rickety, weathered-wood stairs to a narrow deck that couldn't be seen from the front side. Two steel security doors led who-knew-where. *Shouldn't this be storage or something?*

Bryan propped the box he held between the brick wall and his knee, unlocked one door, and shoved it open. He walked in and she heard the box THUMP against the floor, then a click and a snap as the room flooded with light.

A single bare bulb illuminated the room, its pull cord swinging like a pendulum. The square room's brick walls had likely been painted white at one point, but now they were a peeling faded gray. The floor was covered in dust, and cobwebs decorated the corners. In the far corner sat an old door, broken bar stools, and a few empty liquor bottles.

Marlon coughed as he followed his grandfather, setting his box on the floor. "Geez," he said as he headed back out the door, "how many decades has it been since anyone's been in here?"

"Probably not since the sixties," commented Wendel. He sat his box down. "Go ask Sam if we can borrow the broom. In the meantime maybe somebody open a window?"

Abby set her box down. "Sounds like a plan." She walked over and jerked on the rusty latch. After a minute, she'd managed to unlock the window but no amount of effort would get it open.

Bryan joined her. He pulled out his knife and slid the blade between the window and the sill. He used it to lever the window up a couple inches then worked his fingers into the gap and jerked the window open. "There we go, da –" he caught himself "dang thing always stuck."

Abby put her hands on the sill and looked out. The window overlooked the parking lot behind the bar, though it was partly obscured by the short deck. Power poles, scattered trees and distant houses made up the rest of the view. *At least it's better than looking at the back of a building.* Gladys' apartment was on the ground floor, and so the view from her room had been just an alley between the buildings. With a sigh, she turned to go help with the boxes, only to walk into Marlon, now armed with a broom and a dustpan. "Oops, sorry."

"It's OK. Here, you know more about using these than I do."

She took them from him and set the pan on the sill, before trying to combat decades of dust. Once she had a decent pile, she swept it into the pan, then looked around for an empty trash can. When she couldn't find one, she stared at the pan helplessly.

Bryan noticed her dilemma as they came back in. "Just toss the crap out the window," he said as he and Wendel sat the headboard down. "It ain't gonna hurt the blacktop any."

Abby nodded and worked in silence as the Samson boys did the same. At least, she was verbally silent.

"Will you stop acting like becoming more entwined with these people is the best thing that could happen to her?" Aeneas demanded.

"Will you quit acting like it's the worst?" Dominic countered. "She'll be fine. Better than dealing with the Samsons' brand of insanity than the old bat's."

"Dealing with your friend's insane ideas is how you ended up where you are in the first place!"

"You're forgetting the grandson isn't the grandfather."

Will you both knock it off? Abby thought. She almost wished she hadn't unmasked The Dragon. Now that the angel, demon, and her grandfather's ghost no longer had to share the guise to keep their identities hidden, she was a captive audience to all their bickering. Even when the demon was silent, her "good angel" guardians were arguing like an old married couple. *I swear if I'd known what I know now, I'd have never had an imaginary friend.*

Dominic looked up at her with a grin. "Then I'd never have known my favorite granddaughter."

Abby rolled her eyes. *I'm your only granddaughter.*

He chuckled. "Wish I'd only known I was making myself a costume when I made that dang stuffed toy."

She stifled a snicker. *Guess you got too much blood in it from pricking yourself so much.* She sighed. *I'm sorry I lost it.* She hadn't seen the stuffed dragon, the double to the form her grandfather now wore, since before her parents had died twelve years ago.

"We've been over this. It got misplaced, not lost. If it's meant to be, it'll turn up."

"Earth to Abby," called Marlon. "Yo, Abs!"

She turned around and almost dropped the dustpan.

Marlon smiled. "This look all right or you want us to shift some things?"

While she was caught up in the internal conversation, the Samsons had set up her furniture. "How did you?" Despite the surprisingly larger room, everything was in the same position it had been most of her life.

Marlon scratched at the back of his neck with a sheepish grin. "Spent enough time in your room, Abs. Think I know where everything goes."

"Make yourself at home." Wendel looked around the room and shook his head. He shot his father a knowing look. "Not like it's the first time there's been a distressed damsel in here."

Bryan's face turned seven shades of red. "Yeah, yeah, laugh it up, Buzzard." He tipped his hat to Abby and grabbed his son's sleeve. "See ya around, Dragonfly."

"You need anything, you call us." Wendel tossed a cell phone on the bed. "Take care, Abby."

Once they were alone – as far as he knew, as her boyfriend was unaware of her constant companions – Marlon crossed the distance and took her hand. "You gonna be OK, Abs?"

Abby smiled. "Didn't you say I'll be safe here?"

"Being safe and feeling safe are two different things." His thumb rubbed the back of her hand as he looked down at her, his brow creased in concern. "I can crash on the floor…"

"That would be a poor way to reward your Prince Charming. Oughta at least let him share the bed with ya. Though that might lead to an entertaining show…"

Abby flung her arms around Marlon and buried her face in his chest to hide her reaction. She didn't want her boyfriend to misread her irritation and shock at the demon finally putting his two cents in. She supposed the real surprise was that he had waited this long. *Don't you dare make light of this!*

"What's the matter, Abs?" Bjarte's voice was smug, though thankfully that was the only sign of his presence. "The baby bumblebee here came to your rescue just like the knight on his white horse. Even the princess rewarded her champion."

It's Little Wasp, not bumblebee! Abby trembled and Marlon wrapped his arms around her, resting his cheek against the top of her head. She blurted out, "I'll be fine, Mars-Bars. But thank you… for being you."

"You don't look fine, Abs." He stroked her back as if soothing a frightened animal. "You're shaking like a leaf."

"It's been a hard day," she replied. Abby pulled back to meet his worried gaze and shoot him a smile. "I just need to get some sleep I think." She reached into her pocket and held out her car keys. "You better get home. You've got to pick me up and show me how to get to school from here." She rolled her eyes. "Though now that I'm here, pretty sure I could figure it out."

"Better safe than sorry." Marlon sighed, then pressed a quick kiss to her forehead. He gave her a quick, tight hug. "All right, I'm going. But, if you need me, I hooked your laptop up and I'll leave mine on. OK?" He looked her in the eye. "I love you, sleep tight, don't let the bedbugs bite."

"If they do, hit 'em with a shoe and send 'em to the zoo," she replied, laughing at their running joke. "See you in the morning." She leaned close and kissed his cheek. "Love you, too. Always."

Once he was gone, Abby leaned against the door. The sounds of traffic filtered through the open window, and headlights from passing cars chased each other across the floor. She shivered. *I'm alone. Really alone.* Even the one time Gladys had left her on her own, she hadn't truly been by herself. Marlon and his family had been right next door – on both sides.

"Finally got what ya always wanted." Bjarte sounded bored. "Congratulations."

She looked around the room, expecting him to show up somewhere and slow clap. "I'm surprised that's all you have to say," she replied, baiting him. "You were incredibly silent all day. It was nice."

He ignored the jab. "Nice to see you lookin' the part, Cinderelly."

Abby looked down at her dress, groaning at how filthy it was. Now that she was thinking on it, her skin crawled from the dirt covering it. "Ugh… I need a bath."

"Well, it'll have to wait," said Dominic, irritation with the demon's commentary in his voice. "There's no bathroom up here, and you should have been in bed a few hours ago."

The sounds of the city at night continued to make their way into the room. Abby turned and tried to shut the window, which stuck again about halfway down. An abrupt click was her only warning before the light went out. She spun around, stumbling into the boxes stacked up by the door. She just managed to catch herself against the wall. There was a tinkling sound as the old liquor bottles fell out of a cardboard box and shattered against the floor.

"HEY!" yelled Sam from below. "YOU OK UP THERE?"

"YES, SIR!" she called back. "SORRY, I TRIPPED!"

"BE CAREFUL, WILL YA? YA CRACK YOUR HEAD, THOSE WASPS WILL HAVE MINE!"

"YES, SIR! SORRY!" Abby felt her way along the wall to her nightstand and snapped on her lamp. She was unsurprised to find Bjarte leaning against the door with a smirk.

"Cocksure creep," snapped Dominic. "Actin' like ya got power to burn."

"Pride is the vice of his master, after all." Aeneas sounded just as disgusted as Abby felt, but he didn't show himself.

Bjarte snorted. "Geez, you guys never change do you? Killjoys."

Abby went her dresser and pulled open her underwear drawer. She should have been happy Marlon's attention to detail didn't extend to her clothes. Right then though it meant she had to search every drawer just to find one nightgown. *At least I found something to wear tomorrow, too.*

"At least the boy is a gentleman," said Aeneas. "Unlike some I could name."

"I'm going to sleep, so if you all could quit bickering that'd be great." Abby crawled into bed. She managed to change while under the blankets and threw her dirty clothes to the floor. She shut off the lamp and wrapped her covers tightly around her. "Good night!" She felt Dominic jump up on the bed and curl up beside her. His low growl seemed to rumble through the mattress as well as her skin. Comforted, Abby snuggled into her pillow and was almost asleep when....

BANG! THUMP-DA-THUMP!

Something crashed by the window. Jerking up, Abby switched on the lamp.

CHAPTER 5

The first thing she saw was the broom on the floor. Abby sighed. *Must have been the wind.* She was about to shut the light off again when a soft scuffling noise reached her ears. She gulped, threw off the covers and stood up. *It's probably just a mouse, but I'll never be able to sleep if I don't know for sure.* She followed the noise to the boxes by the window.

Eyes locked on the boxes, she picked up the broom, her hand shaking. As weapons went, it was a poor choice, but it was all she had. She used the handle to push the boxes aside, flinching at the hiss they made as they slid across the floor. A ball of dusty black fur moved and she raised the broom over her head, ready to strike. But just as she stared to bring it down...

"Mew?" The furball tumbled and rolled onto its side, looking up at her with pale yellow eyes.

"Shh, little one," she said, kneeling and slowly laying the broom on the floor. She crawled closer as the kitten, at most eight weeks old she thought, hissed and spit. She reached out and caught hold of its scruff, her fingers brushing ragged nylon. She looked the kitten over and realized the collar was wrapped tight around its right foreleg. "Poor baby." She stood up, tucking the kitten against her chest, supporting its feet. "I'll get that off."

"How did it even get up here?" asked Dominic, following her over to her desk. He watched as she took her scissors from the plastic tumbler on her desk and worked to chop the ratty collar off.

"No idea," she said, peeling the collar away from where it had grown into the kitten's skin. Who knew how long it had been walking around on only three legs. She lightly stroked the dirty black fur. "Shhh, there we go, baby. There we go." Lifting the now-much-calmer kitten into her arms, she cradled it much as she once had her childhood cat, Troubadour. "It's OK, you're safe now."

The kitten looked up at her and purred.

Abby sat down on the bed, rocking the kitten as she found herself smiling. After Troubadour had died, Gladys had refused to let her get another cat. And she never would have allowed her to have a black one like this little furball. Looking closer, she noticed two white spots on its belly... and the fact he was obviously a boy. "Aren't you a cute little fuzzy-wuzzy?"

"Gag me with a spoon," said Bjarte, leaning against the wall, his arms and ankles crossed. "I guess you needed to complete the gig. After all, you already have the broom. Now you just need the pointed hat."

Abby felt a hand squeeze her shoulder. Aeneas's silent but unquestionable presence, on top of Dominic's low growling, was enough to allow her to ignore the demon. She tickled the kitten, smiling as he grabbed her fingers, biting but not actually breaking the skin. "Pretty sure Sam won't mind if I keep you. He seemed nice enough, even if he is a bit gruff."

"Besides, Little Wasp would complain if he said no," said Dominic, chuckling.

She laughed, picturing Marlon's reaction. He always understood and had helped her find Troubadour the few times he'd escaped. "You'll need a name."

From the window the sound of music echoed as a car passed by, a familiar song playing on its radio. Van Morrison's soft voice called to mind memories of dancing in the kitchen with her parents. The song's title went right along with the white dots on the kitten's belly.

"Whoa-oh," Abby sang softly. "Domino."

Dominic gave her an incredulous look. "Domino," he repeated, having picked up her train of thought. "Dom-in-o. Seriously?"

"Well," said Aeneas, materializing beside her on the bed. The angel wore a rare smirk. "Look at it this way: should she say 'Dommy' aloud, it would be assumed to be the cat she was talking to." He reached out and lightly tapped the kitten's nose.

Dominic rolled his eyes. He climbed back onto the bed and curled up beside Abby's pillow. "I guess I'm lucky she didn't name him 'Dragon'."

Aeneas vanished as he chuckled.

Abby sighed and slid back under the blankets, the kitten tucked under her chin, and fell asleep to the sound of purring for the first time in years.

A loud pounding on the door forced Abby out of bed. She looked at the window and groaned. *It's not even light out.* She pushed off the blankets and the chill of the room sliced through her gown. She flinched as her bare feet hit the ice-cold floor, making a mental note to find her slippers as soon as possible. She clutched Domino tight and walked over to the door, peeking out the curtain to see Sam standing in the dim light. She unlocked the door and opened it. "Morning, sir."

"Just wanted to give ya this," Sam said, shoving a key into her hand. He looked at the kitten and smirked. "Two strays in one night? Haven't had that happen in a couple decades. Anyway, there's a shower downstairs between the kitchen and the storeroom. You can use it until Queenie's people get here and fix ya up." He rolled his eyes and tried to imitate Marlon's grandmother. "I swear, you expect a lady to manage without proper facilities?"

Dominic chuckled. "Leave it to Wasp's lady."

Abby laughed, too. "That sounds like Mrs. Samson. Thank you, sir." She shifted Domino in her arms. "Is it alright if I keep him? He sorta fell in the window last night."

"Just keep him inside. He's lucky he ain't roadkill." Sam turned and crossed the deck to the door beside her own. "You wanna catch a shower before your man gets here, I'd hustle."

Abby thanked him again and shut the door, letting Domino down. She went over to her trunk and opened it. In a few minutes she had Troubadour's old crate set up by her bed, complete with litter box and bowls. *Good thing I never threw his stuff away.* The litter was old, but it would do until she could get more. "You just need some water and food..."

"There are two stores next door," said Dominic, watching as she sat the kitten in the crate and latched the door. "Doubt they're open this early though."

She picked up her bottle of water from the nightstand and poured it in the kitten's bowl. "I'm sorry buddy, I'll get you something to eat as soon as I can." At least he was safe for the moment. "I can't even remember the last time I emptied this thing," she said, rummaging through her trunk and finding a few cat toys buried under her photo albums. She sighed. Even if she had lucked out and found a can of food in the mess, it wouldn't be safe to feed him anyway. "I'll see if I can get away at lunch and bring you something."

"Goin' hungry one day won't kill him. And locked up like that he can't go chowing down on any cords."

Abby ignored Bjarte's smug voice and searched her drawers for a clean outfit. She found a cotton dress and shoes, then threw on her robe before she headed downstairs. She could at least wash off and change. It felt too chilly to get her hair wet since she didn't have a hair dryer. "Or a washcloth," she muttered as she stepped into the restroom. She locked the door.

"Sam told you where the shower is," Dominic pointed out. He closed his eyes when she stripped and ran a paper towel under the tap before washing off with it.

"I know, but I don't know where the kitchen is and I don't need to be late." She dried off, pulled her clothes on, and threw her backpack over her shoulder before tucking her nightgown and robe under her arm. She went back outside and locked up, putting the key in her pocket.

"Good morning, beautiful."

"Mars-Bars!" Abby shrieked. She glared at Marlon where he stood, leaning against the front of her car. She loosened her grip on her sleepwear in relief. "Don't do that!"

Marlon scratched his chin with a sheepish expression and held out a paper sack. "Figured you'd need breakfast."

Abby smiled as she took the bag in her free hand. "Come on, there's someone I want you to meet." She led the way back up the stairs and unlocked her door. She tossed her sleepwear on the bed then walked over to the cage. Abby pulled the sandwich out of the sack and tore it in half before poking what passed for egg and cheese through the bars. "Meet Domino."

"He's a cute little guy." Marlon joined her as the kitten wolfed down the food. He reached into his pocket and held out her keys. "Wish I'd brought another sandwich. That'll take the edge off for him, but it won't help you much."

"I'll be fine." Abby took the keys and added the two new ones to the ring. "We better get going. Last thing I need is to be late to class and give them more to talk about."

CHAPTER 6

"I wonder why everyone was surprised the Samsons came to the rescue."

"What are you talking about?" Abby looked up as Melissa sat down beside her in study hall, grinning ear to ear.

Melissa looked at her sideways. "Well, for starters, Drew did talk to his dad about Gladys' nonsense. Of course, his father said that he'd suggested the action to her."

"He did what?" The words came out before Abby could stop them, in unison with Aeneas and Dominic. *Dommy*, she said silently as The Dragon started growling, *please calm down!* She wasn't sure if she was more shocked or furious herself.

"That self-righteous, pompous..." Dominic rambled on as Melissa explained.

"Apparently it was supposed to be a scare tactic. He said she couldn't legally give you only forty-eight hours' notice, but you wouldn't know that. Before Drew could say anything about how stupid that was, the phone rang. Guess who?"

Abby groaned. "Aunt Gladys, telling him it backfired and those 'wolves in sheep's clothing' had taken me and my things away, aided by her fallen sister."

"Pretty much. You should have heard Dolores trying to calm Gladys down." Melissa smiled, amused as a kitten with a catnip toy. "I'm supposed to tell you to come home, she's worried sick about you. Keywords: *Supposed to.*"

Dominic's rant stopped and he burst out laughing.

"I take it you're not going to?" Abby smiled and pulled out her notebook as the teacher came in.

"Nope," said Melissa. She smiled back. "It's about time you were free of that controlling witch. But I want details. All anyone said at lunch was Mr. Samson and his father took care of it. Spill!"

"You're as much a gossip as your mother-in-law," Abby teased before gave her friend a rundown of what happened. "Then when I was trying to sleep, this black kitten fell in the window," she finished. "He's a cute little fellow. I'm just glad I kept Troubadour's things."

"Remind me to never get on Mr. Samson's bad side," said Melissa, swapping her math book for the literature one. She smiled. "Though Mrs. Lynde earned it."

"Mr. Samson doesn't hurt friends, Mel."

"I know. So what did you name the kitten?" She giggled. "Troubadour Two?"

"Domino," replied Abby, smiling. She ignored Dominic's snort. "I have to get him some food, though."

"The dollar store should have some," said Melissa. She smiled. "So you're gonna be a barmaid, huh? Should I start calling you Carla?"

Abby rolled her eyes. "Sam looks more like Coach, but if Cliff and Norm come in I'll let you know." The bell rang and they scrambled to get to their next class.

Abby parked the Monte Carlo behind the bar. She slung on her backpack then reached over and pulled the kitten food from the passenger seat. After a quick trip upstairs to feed Domino and to put her backpack on the desk, she bolted back downstairs to report for work. *I've no idea what I'm supposed to do or how long I'm working,* she realized. When she voiced these concerns to Sam, he pulled an envelope out from under the bar and handed it to her.

"Buzzard's lady brought that in this morning. She did the job herself once upon a time. Ya start this Friday." He shook his head and went back to cleaning the bar. "Your future mother-in-law oughtta have covered everything but you have any questions, ask 'em."

Abby sputtered and just barely managed to thank him before she escaped upstairs to her room. Inside the envelope she found a letter from Marlon's mother, a list of do's and don'ts, a shorthand code for orders, translation for common names for drinks with a note that if asked for any of these, to explain she couldn't serve them, and the work schedule. She sat the information on her desk and got started on her homework. "It looks easy enough. Wish I could say the same about this assignment."

"So, no comment on the assumption you'll be walking down the aisle with Little Wasp?"

Abby glared at Dominic. "We're *eighteen*, OK? It's way too early to be thinking about that."

"Didn't stop Drew the rat and Mel," he noted, stretching out beside her on the floor. "They seem pretty happy with the situation."

"Drew's parents were just scared he and Mel might have sex or something." Abby rolled her eyes. "Gee, I guess the idea of people having self-control is too far-fetched."

Dominic looked at her, tapping his tail against the floor. His smirk annoyed her. "Methinks the lady doth protest too much."

"She'll likely end up pullin' a Jacob-Rachel-Leah with Prince Charming and one of his siblings." Bjarte appeared, seated on her desk. "Personally, think the sister would be the more interesting option. I mean if you're gonna live in sin, go all the way."

"Your mind is little more than a backed-up sewer," Aeneas replied, actually showing himself for a change, arms folded across his chest and a look of complete disgust on his face.

Abby choked. She put her head in her hands and tried in vain to get the images the demon's words had painted out of her mind. That Marlon's uncle had fathered Marlon's brothers was common knowledge, and half of why her aunt and Preacher Davidson were so against the Samsons. "It doesn't work like that." She jerked her thumb over her shoulder at the demon. "I'm trying to work here, so take a hike, Wormwood."

"What was it ya said to that blond chick? Somethin' about not havin' to work?" Bjarte's grin sent a chill down her spine. "Could be you, too. Just have to 'yolk yourself with a non-believer'."

"Marlon knows almost as much as I do about being Catholic," Abby snapped. "Look, I never said I don't want to marry him, I said it's too soon to think about it!"

"He goes 'cause it's the only way he'll ever get in between your legs."

Abby grabbed her textbook and swung it at the demon, forgetting that he wasn't solid. Her swing went right through him and she lost her balance, falling halfway out of her chair. Bjarte's laughter ran in her ears as she forced herself upright. When she looked again, he was gone.

"Head games," said Dominic, growling. "Nothing more, nothing less."

Abby nodded and got back to work. "I know."

CHAPTER 7

"OK, so the napkins came in this afternoon, and the coasters…" Abby shuffled the paperwork on Sam's ancient desk, putting invoices into one pile and bills into another. She looked at the inventory sheet she'd drawn up on her laptop, checking to make sure everything was accounted for. She wasn't sure if she was relieved or not that, according to Sam, she would only have to "work the floor" when they were busy. Otherwise, her job was to "deal with the paperwork." A ding from the laptop caught her attention and Abby looked over to see her messenger window open.

RandomWord: How's it goin', beautiful?

DragonflyGirl: Slow but steady. How about you?

RandomWord: Trying to find out more about this one college. This town seriously lacks video game design degree programs. Hey, I got something to show you. What do you think?

Abby clicked the file he sent, and choked.

"Whoa, the boy's got talent!" Bjarte's laughter echoed in her ears. "Only thing he screwed up is Annie actually looks like he doesn't have his staff up his –"

Shut up! Abby clicked the X to close the picture harder than the task required. She went back to the messenger and typed, "Why are you drawing the characters from Grandpa Nick's game?"

RandomWord: After what you said on your birthday about wanting to make it a public game, I thought I'd see what concepts I could come up with.

Abby didn't know how to respond. It wasn't his fault that her angel and demon had also been her grandfather's. Or that they shared

PATH OF THE DRAGON

their appearances with the game's characters. She flinched at the next message.

RandomWord: I didn't … look I didn't mean to overstep, Abs, I wasn't sure I could pull it off. You like or should I scrap?

DragonflyGirl: You're talented, Mars-Bars. But I can't talk about this right now. I'm working and Sam's filing system requires a lot of concentration.

RandomWord: Right, sorry, just… Yeah. Love you, Abs. Talk to you later?

DragonflyGirl: *smiles* Of course Mars-Bars. I love you, too. Check ya later.

She closed the window after Marlon signed off, and went back to the paperwork. She glanced down at The Dragon at her feet. *How do you feel about the concepts?*

"Little Wasp did a good job," said Dominic, picking up on her concerns. "If you really expect to get that game out there, it might need updating you know."

It's the last thing you worked on, she replied. She started copying her spreadsheet onto the one Sam had given her to fill out. *It should stay as you made it.*

"Won't do it much good if it doesn't go anywhere." The Dragon laid his head on his paws. "And it can't make a difference then."

As much as she wanted to leave it as is, it was his game. Still… *Getting it revamped will probably be expensive.* Abby sighed as she laid the paperwork out for Sam to check later. "I'm gonna need to get a printer."

"Good plan, give you more time for foolin' around with Prince Charmin'." Bjarte had yet to make himself visible, which she suspected he was doing on purpose since it made her jumpy. "Be more fun now that you don't have to hide anythin' from the old bat."

Get thee behind me, Wormwood. Abby closed her laptop and left the office, shutting off the light and locking the door behind her. She gave Sam back the key before she went upstairs.

Domino was climbing the side of the crate, meowing his delight at her return. Or maybe he was just saying "Let me out!"

Abby set the laptop on her bed, open – in case Marlon messaged again – then let the kitten out to play. She rolled a ping-pong ball between her feet, laughing as Domino did his best to catch it.

"You know, the only downside to this place is Prince Charmin' can't sneak in your window anymore. Shame, as you could play a few different games now."

Abby gritted her teeth. She *did* miss having Marlon right next door, but not for the reasons the demon thought. Knowing he was a message away and would be there if she needed him... while she didn't need a "white knight," she did need her best friend. Her laptop dinged right on cue. She smiled at the message.

RandomWord: You doin' OK, Abs?

DragonflyGirl: Yeah, just playing with Domino. How about you?

RandomWord: I'm taking a break from packing. Apparently, Mrs. Lynde won't have to put up with us much longer either. Dad talked Uncle Richie into moving out, too. *sighs* The place has gotten too small since Isaac was born. Now that he's crawling into everything...

Abby fidgeted, not wanting to worry. As if sensing her discomfort, Domino leapt up onto the bed and curled up against her, purring. She gently stroked the kitten for a moment. Finally she typed, "So changing schools again?"

RandomWord: Naw, the new place is only a block from where you're at. You're stuck with me, beautiful. Though this is gonna be a ride. Uncle Richie, Miss Xandi and Nina are moving in with us. So I guess we really will be a TV show.

Dominic chuckled. "Sounds about right. Or a soap opera."

"Aunt Gladys asked for it," said Abby, smiling. She typed, "Be careful what you wish for, you just might get it, I guess. Gladys' wanted you guys out, she got it."

RandomWord: Yeah, and you with us. *grins* So you gonna be on the forum tomorrow? Or can I talk you into lunch?

DragonflyGirl: How about we grab a couple cheeseburgers and hang out here for a bit? I kinda miss the monkey climbing in my window.

RandomWord: *laughs* You got it Abs. I'll bring my laptop. Speaking of which, how'd your first day go?

DragonflyGirl: Slow but could have been a lot worse. I just hope I didn't destroy Sam's organization. Got time for a chess match or do you gotta get back to packing?

RandomWord: Packing sadly. Raincheck?

DragonflyGirl: Always. Love you, Mars-Bars.

RandomWord: Right back at ya, Abs. See ya tomorrow.

Abby shutdown the laptop, then got up and sat it on her desk. She plugged it in to charge, then stroked the case. *It's weird to be able to leave this out. Years of hiding up in smoke.*

"Free at last, free at last, thank God Almighty you're free at last!" Bjarte laughed. "You're thinking so small though, Abs. You're of age! Live a little!"

Domino pawed the hem of her skirt, meowing for her to pick him up.

Abby lifted him up, then turned on her CD player. DC Talk filled the room and she started to dance with the kitten. Abby laughed when he nipped her nose. She spun around and came face-to-face with Bjarte.

"Can I cut in?" The smirk was unnerving.

Abby bit back a shriek of surprise. Her eyes narrowed. "No, thank you." She glanced at the clock, then put Domino back in his crate. She got out pajamas and took refuge in her makeshift changing room. After some trial and error, the old door, a couple heavy crates, and a shower curtain gave her the illusion of privacy. She ignored Bjarte's wolf-whistle.

But her guardians didn't. Dominic's low growl came from the other side of the curtain along with Aeneas' scolding. "You have no decency at all!"

"Why, thank you!" Bjarte laughed. "How nice of you to notice."

Abby tossed her clothes into the basket by the door, took Domino back out of the crate, wrapped the two of them in the blankets and shut off her lamp. "If Marlon's life is a soap opera, mine's some SciFi channel special. Goodnight." She turned up her CD just enough to drown them out and drifted off to sleep.

CHAPTER 8

Abby woke to the rattle of kibble hitting plastic and Domino leaping over her to get to his food dish. She sat up and found Marlon pouring water into the other bowl, a tied up plastic sack beside him. "What the... Mars-Bars, how did you get in here?"

"Window." He gently scratched the kitten's ears before shooting her a grin. "We're gonna have to get you a screen for that."

Abby rubbed her eyes. "You actually got it open from the outside?" She had bought a can of oil when she got the cat food, and had managed to almost completely shut the window. The tiny gap that was left, she kept covered with a towel.

"Yeah, you left it open a crack." He scratched at the back of his neck sheepishly. "Uh, no offense, Abs, but if you're gonna do that, we need to get a brace for the window. If I can do it, anybody else could, too."

Her sleep-fogged brain reacted to that sentence like she'd been covered in ice water. When she'd gotten the window down but then couldn't move it either direction, she'd assumed it was stuck good and no one would be able to move it. *It was like that all week!*

Marlon caught her expression. "Don't worry about it, Abs, I'll get a brace before I head home today. Maybe I can talk Grandma into making Sam replace it. I mean, I get it, it's always been like that, but that was then and this is now."

Abby started to get out of bed, but before she could move the blanket...

41

"Whoo-hoo!" Bjarte appeared behind Marlon, smirking knowingly. "That's more like it, give the poor boy something for his trouble!"

She reacted before she could think about it. Abby grabbed her pillow and threw it at the demon, only for it to smack straight into her boyfriend. She scrambled to cover the slip up. "Mars-Bars!" she shouted. "Do you realize I'm not even dressed yet?"

Marlon's face flushed red. He quickly picked up the pillow and tossed it back on her bed. "Sorry Abs, just you were talkin' about the window thing and -" he cut himself off "- look I'll just go outside while ya change. Dang it, sorry I swear I didn't even -" The rest of his words were incomprehensible as he locked Domino in the cage and bolted out the door.

Abby sighed, feeling terrible. Yes, it *was* wrong that he'd pretty much broken into her room, but she knew he didn't mean any harm. She narrowed her eyes at the demon. *You... GO AWAY! I am not going to fall for your tricks, I don't want to serve your "boss," I'm not interested in what you're selling, so take a hike already!*

"Oh, come on. Tell me that stunt isn't every girl's dream." Bjarte rolled his eyes and followed her behind the screen. He leaned up against the wall and gave her a seductive smile. "Ya know... if it's the kids thing you're worried about... I could help ya relieve some stress..."

Dominic's roar echoed in her ears. "I'll be damned before you lay a hand on her!"

Abby turned her back on the demon, trying to pretend she didn't understand what he was saying. She changed her clothes as quickly as she could, but her skin crawled as the feeling of exposure she'd learned to tune out came back full-force. She tried hard to forget that the demon did get some sick thrill out of watching her. Granted she wasn't sure if it was sexual or just a power rush.

"Be careful what ya say and who ya say it to, ya overgrown gecko."

Ignoring the chill the demon's words sent down her spine, Abby went outside to find Marlon leaning against the railing of the small porch outside her and Sam's doors. She carefully moved beside him and laid her hand on his. "Sorry, I overreacted…"

"No you didn't, Abs. You always let me in before." Marlon turned his hand over and laced his fingers through hers. "I am gonna do something about that window. There's been a lot of sh—er, stuff going on lately and…" He sighed. "I'm glad you don't have to put up with your aunt these days, but I wish I was closer."

The wind picked up and Abby shivered. "You're close enough." She lightly kissed his cheek. "Come on, let's get inside."

"Abs, I swear, you keep sharing your food with him, I'll have to start getting him his own meals."

Abby held out another French fry to Domino. "It's just a couple fries. Besides," she smiled as he wolfed it down, "it wouldn't be fair to leave him out."

Marlon just smiled and shook his head from where he lay on his stomach beside her on her bed. "You're in Seventh Heaven now that you have a cat again." He crumpled up the wrapper to his burger and box from his fries then tossed both into the trash can.

So, Dominic privately said, *where do you think Wormwood ran off to this time?*

Aeneas looked over at Dominic, his former charge, where he lay on the pillows, watching his granddaughter and her suitor. *I wish I knew. He never does anything without reason.*

Dominic growled. *His mind games are getting old fast.* His claws kneaded the pillow beneath them. *You saw how she snapped today. He keeps this up, one of these days she won't be able to just play it off.*

43

He lost a good deal of leverage when she left Davidson's fold, Aeneas replied. He folded his arms and leaned against the wall by the headboard. *He is scrambling to make up for it.*

Dominic snorted. *You've misjudged him before. Doesn't look to me like he needs leverage. He's planting seeds, and when they sprout we're gonna have a ton of weeding to do.*

What seeds he is sowing mostly fall by the wayside, Aeneas told him. He couldn't show his own doubts. *She has support, even if it is less than desirable... It is still better than Mrs. Lynde doing his work for him.*

Wasp and his family aren't what landed me in the slammer and you know it. Dominic sighed. *Wanting to protect my little girl did. Right now, all she has to protect are Little Wasp and that kitten. If she didn't change her morals after a decade with the old bat, she won't now.*

I hope you're right, replied the guardian. *For all our sakes.*

CHAPTER 9

Abby sat beside Marlon in a back row pew. Now and then she noticed he couldn't seem to sit still, but that was normal. Mass wasn't Davidson's judgmental services. They didn't have to keep up appearances anymore. She would have never in a million years expected Marlon to attend Mass with her. Yes, he had made a promise. *But I don't need support here. Why does he think he needs to listen to what his whole family believes is a poorly written fairy tale?*

"Love is blind," said Dominic from his place at her feet tucked under the pew.

Are you trying to sound like Aeneas? she thought at The Dragon. *Cryptic spiritual commentary coming from you makes me wonder who's wearing the mask.*

"We can talk later." The Dragon tapped his claws against the floor. "If you're going to have your head in the clouds, you might as well stay home."

You started the... Abby stopped herself. Arguing with elders was impossible to win, dead or alive. Father Steve wrapped up the homily and the Mass came to an end. As usual, she walked out the door feeling refreshed, though a bit hungry. True to her memory of Sundays with her parents, she never ate before Mass.

Marlon tossed his pink – salmon, Abby corrected herself – sweater into the back seat as they got into her car. His hand went to the radio automatically and switched to the rock station.

Abby started the car. "You know you don't have to –"

"– come to Mass with you," he finished. He got his sketch pad out of the glove box and started drawing. "How many times are we gonna have this conversation, Abs? I made a promise. I'm keeping it. End of story."

She sighed and changed the subject. "Where do you want to go for breakfast?"

Marlon didn't look up from his drawing. "I don't care where I am so long as I'm with you." He spun the pencil around and started erasing a few lines. "Burger joint or the Ritz, all the same to me." She worried he'd leave it at that, but then he added, "Think that one buffet place is open down the street here, though."

Abby smiled then looked back as she pulled out of the parking space. She thought back to the slip up the day before. *I shouldn't have snapped at him. But how else could I have covered that up?* She considered it as she waited to exit the parking lot. *Guess I could have started a pillow fight.*

"And given Wormwood a free show."

What am I supposed to do? Abby snapped mentally at her grandfather's ghost as she felt her face heat up. She made herself focus on pulling out into the busy street. *He's not going anywhere, I can't lock him out. What do you want me to do, join the Dominican Sisters? It's not like neither you nor Aeneas are going to give me privacy either.*

"You OK, Abs?" Marlon reached out and felt her forehead. "You look hot. You aren't coming down with something are you?"

She smiled at the concern in his voice. "I'm fine." *So long as you're here, I'm fine.*

Abby woke up and groaned at the sun coming in the windows. *Forgot to shut the curtains again.* After a few weeks of her new routine, Abby was drained. Friday night she'd flopped straight into bed. If not for the insistent demands for food and attention from the increasingly

46

larger Domino, she wouldn't consider moving from that spot before dawn. As it was, she did good to tend to his basic needs before she crashed. Yesterday had been no exception. The bar had been packed with people raising a glass to those lost eight years before. *I am never drinking, I swear.*

If nothing else, working for Sam had cemented her belief that alcohol made people make stupid mistakes. She had lost track of how many times she'd been hit on or been asked for orders she had told them a thousand times she couldn't fill. Plus she'd slipped and landed on her rear when someone forgot to tell her they'd spilled their pitcher. When Sam told her to clock out, the relief had to have been written all over her face.

On the plus side, between her and Marlon's grandmother, she was finally starting to feel at home. The room now boasted not only a bathroom, but a hot plate, microwave, and mini-fridge. After several thrift store trips, she had turned a few cabinets and a table into a kitchenette. Her TV stand and its occupants had a space all to itself with a rug spread on the floor in front of it. She still hadn't made any progress finding chairs, but Marlon, Felice, and Melissa were usually content to sit on the floor or her trunk.

As much as she didn't want to get up, it was Saturday. And Saturday was spent on Friday's homework and whatever time she had left went to the online forum. Over the two years she'd been playing the role of Ava Crewe on the forum, Abby had made some good friends. *Just would be nice if they lived closer.* Then again, she usually joked that even if they met in person, they'd all just retreat to their laptops anyway. With a sigh, she forced herself out of bed.

"Meow!" Domino rubbed along her ankles as she got out his food, refilled both his bowls and cleaned the litterbox. She stroked his head before starting on her homework. She was researching a paper when her messenger flew open.

RandomWord: Abs, quick hit the Sanctuary. You aren't gonna believe this!

DragonflyGirl: Marlon, I'm in the middle of my homework here. The game can wait a few minutes. *rolls eyes* Sometimes all you think about is games.

RandomWord: Drew just axed his character.

Abby stared at the message in confusion. "What do you mean?" she typed. "Drew hasn't been on since he started college."

RandomWord: Haven't checked your email lately have you? The Queens sent a notice out two days ago stating that… hold on, I'll copy.

Abby went back to her research while she waited. She couldn't let her grades slip just because she was tired.

RandomWord: Here we go. "Please note that as per the updated guidelines, any player whose character holds up a thread for more than a month will receive a warning and action will be taken to move the thread along. After three such warnings the player will be banned from the site permanently. If you are aware you are going to be gone, it is only respectful to your fellow players that you do not make posts that prevent your fellow players from enjoying the game."

"The kid's gotta be making this up," said Dominic, standing up on his hind legs to look at the screen. "That would have to be against the rules, wouldn't it?"

Abby repeated The Dragon's question to Marlon. When Marlon didn't answer right away, she knew this was bad. She clicked her shortcut to the forum and scrolled straight down to the chatbox.

JennerTheRat: Will you get off my case? I took care of the problem didn't I?

GreenQueen: You're being a puppy just because some reasonable rules were

JennerTheRat: Reasonable rules my hand. You haven't made a reasonable ch

WaterHorse: The boy's in college. There's such a thing as responsibilities and

GreenQueen: Yeah, right. Way he's acting I'd be surprised if he's not still in grade

Abby shook her head. Ever since the chatbox had been upgraded it was impossible to type more than a couple sentences at a time. It was one of many "upgrades" that had been done without user consent. They happened, you complained, then learned to adjust or quit playing. Plenty of people had come and gone since she had joined. At least once she and Marlon had tried to set up a group chat – only for her laptop to have a hissy fit. So they stayed and played the game, though they talked a few times of finding another site to chat.

Abby tried a couple more times to make sense of the chat then gave up. *The drunks were more sensible.*

Marlon finally came back to their usual chat. "That stupid box makes having a real conversation impossible," the message read. "Don't even bother trying to make sense of it."

DragonflyGirl: Too late, already did. *sighs* I remember when you told me not to argue with her, and she's just gotten worse. Why doesn't someone report her to WhiteQueen?

RandomWord: Love to, but can't. She's on hiatus indefinitely. Got a family member sick and needs to go help out or something, has no idea when she'll be back.

DragonflyGirl: And yet, Drew's inactivity is a problem?

RandomWord: My thoughts exactly.

DragonflyGirl: This is such a mess. I'll be on after I finish my homework. Hopefully they'll calm down by then.

RandomWord: *snorts* Good luck with that. I'll keep an eye on the chat, but I swear it makes as much sense as the messages from the Ruins of Alph.

Abby rolled her eyes at the reference. "See ya later, Mars-Bars," she replied, then went back to her homework.

CHAPTER 10

Ava was grateful cats couldn't cry as she followed Brock and the others away from the screams of pain that cut off all too abruptly. Their friend was gone, and she made a private vow that his sacrifice would not be in vain. He would be avenged one day, somehow. But it was hard to see how with their resources thin as they were. They were marked now, known, and their only hope for escape was a path guarded by the dead. The Ragdoll cat gulped then forced herself into the storm drain after her friends and down into the catacombs beneath the city. Her whole body recoiled from the feel of standing upon the piles of human bones, but she kept close to Brock, unwilling to get lost down in this hidden city of ghosts.

Abby sadly shook her head. In two years, her writing had improved some, but was still melodramatic. In this case she felt it was warranted. Drew was gone. Not just the in-game character Harley Lawrence - Drew. The chat was an unreadable mess, but she could see he had been banned from the forum. His profile picture was gone, his name was black, and his basic name, not what he had changed it too, was visible. On all his posts. She couldn't tell what had happened for sure - had he actually said something to earn it? You couldn't find the context in the chat if you were an English major. She kept refreshing the page, waiting for a reply to her post. Finally one appeared and it took every ounce of self-control not to knock the laptop off the table.

After dispatching the rat that had dared to challenge her, Tremo Light followed the scent trail its companions had left behind. She paused at the narrow opening that led beneath the city. She curled a lip in disgust at their foolishness. They would never escape that maze. "They're as good as dead down there, and if they come back, we'll kill 'em." She kicked some dirt into the hole and turned back to report to her contacts.

(OOC: Don't be getting any wise ideas. He did it to himself; anyone that disagrees with his punishment, speak now and join him, or get over it and move on. I catch any more hidden threats in posts and the offender will be banned on the spot.)

Abby stared at the post. She opened the messenger and contacted Marlon. "Did she really just take an in-character comment as a THREAT?"

RandomWord: What did you expect, Abs? You know how she is. WhiteQueen was the only one to reign her in. I'm half-expecting to see the "rebellion" quieted real fast. I mean you saw how fast "Jade" ratted out the Society once she was "captured."

DragonflyGirl: Yeah wasn't that just priceless, since she asked everyone "will you guard the secrets under threat of torture". *snorts* Practice what you preach much?

RandomWord: *laughs* I hear ya. What's worse is White left Green's puppet in her place. She's not gonna say a word about this crap.

Abby sighed then replied, "I don't like this one bit. The game's been going downhill for a while now. It's like only the Queens' private club counts. Everyone else, they don't care about at all. Remind me again why we're here?"

RandomWord: Because you own a piece-of-junk-laptop you bought for a couple hundred in a thrift store. You know Abs, you can get a new one for the same price? Dad could move all your stuff I'll bet. Then you could chat without the forum.

DragonflyGirl: The money my parents left isn't as much as I thought it was. The college fund is intact and should get me through as far as tuition and books goes, but I'm gonna have to be careful with the rest.

RandomWord: You have a job now. You're covered.

A job your family got me. It wasn't that she wasn't grateful. She knew they only wanted to help her. But it was like there hadn't even been a problem. She had dealt with plenty on her own – right down to the mystery of what her imaginary friend really was. In some ways it was nice to have someone come rushing in to the rescue, but...

"But you're not helpless." Dominic got off the bed and sat beside her. "You're not the princess locked in the tower held captive by the dragon waiting for the prince to come. You've already slayed the dragon and went on your way."

"He's fine with me making my own choices," she said softly, "so long as it's not about the solution to my problems." She stroked Domino when he climbed up into her lap.

"I believe you mean she tamed the dragon." Aeneas' voice held amusement. She felt his hand squeeze her shoulder. "Tell him. He will understand."

RandomWord: Abs? Sorry, I didn't mean to... I dunno, just you shouldn't have to deal with this crap. I know you only put up with it because of our friends, but...

DragonflyGirl: I'll live. I don't have to put up with it all the time like I did with Aunt Gladys.

RandomWord: Valid point.

BuzzardBreath: Not to cut in, but since SOMEONE forgot to relay his mother's message: You mind coming over for lunch tomorrow Abby? Everyone's missin' ya.

RandomWord: DAD!

Abby laughed. She startled Domino, who looked up at her like she'd lost her mind. She scratched the kitten's ears and tried to force herself to stop. Just when she nearly had herself under control, though...

BuzzardBreath: I know I'm not interrupting anything indecent, son. So I fail to see your complaint.

RandomWord: THAT'S NOT THE POINT! WE WERE TALKING HERE!

BuzzardBreath: And if you had delivered a message, I wouldn't be doing it instead.

DragonflyGirl: I'll be there Mr. Samson. But right now, I need to get to sleep. Night, Mars-Bars. I love you. *blows kiss*

"You're terrible," snickered Dominic.

"I know." Abby grinned. "Three… two… one."

RandomWord: *catches to keep for later* Sleep well, Abs, love you too.

BuzzardBreath: Awww! *screenshots* LOL Thanks Abby I'll tell Tura. Night you love birds.

RandomWord: DAD! Dammit!

Abby snickered as she shut the laptop off and got ready for bed. She waited for the commentary from Bjarte, and was not relieved when it didn't come. *Wormwood's been pretty quiet,* she thought, silently asking for confirmation from her guardians. *I don't like it.*

"That would make two of us," Aeneas admitted.

"Three," chimed in Dominic. He climbed onto the bed and curled beside her on the other pillow. "There's nothing we can do but wait. Whatever he's up to, it'll come when it comes."

She cradled Domino and wrapped them in the blankets, then silently said her prayers before drifting off to sleep.

CHAPTER 11

"You've really settled in fast." Abby trailed after Marlon's mother. It was just after lunch and Abby was getting a tour of their house. "It's impressive."

Datura averted her eyes. "Thank you. It's good for the kids to have room to move finally."

As if summoned by the indirect mention, Marlon's youngest brother came running up, clutching a pillow. "Ah-bee!" he cried, clinging to her, then hiding behind her. "Ah-bee, save meee!"

"Save you from what, Isaac?" She picked up the pillow he'd dropped so he could cling to her skirt. "Why are you dragging this around, anyway?"

"You get back here with my pillow you little sh-!" Kenny skidded to a stop and looked up at his mother with a sheepish expression. "Heh heh, I mean, please give my pillow back."

Abby bit her tongue to keep from laughing and handed it over.

"Thanks." Kenny looked at Isaac in annoyance. "How come I gotta share a room with that brat? All he does is think up new ways to torture me."

"Marlon has to share with him, too, and he has to put up with both of you," replied his mother, rubbing her forehead. "He's still learning boundaries. You need to be firm with him."

"Marlon escapes to Grandpa's or Abby's." Kenny started strangling the pillow as he looked at Isaac darkly. "Last time I was firm with him, I was grounded."

"Firm doesn't mean locking him in the closet!"

"But what if they needed him in Narnia?"

A hand reached out and caught her shoulder, and Abby turned to find Wendel gesturing for her to follow. She gently disengaged from Isaac and obliged.

"Life's a happy chaos, gotta admit," he said, leading her into what she expected to be his office, but found to be both office and bedroom. He gestured for her to have a seat at the desk as he went to the closet. "Good to finally have everyone under one roof again."

Abby looked around, noticing the family photos that all but completely covered the walls. "On one hand, you've got more room than you had but on the other…" She tilted her head in confusion when he came back with a scrapbook. "What is it? Baby pictures of Mars-Bars?"

Wendel chuckled. "Pretty sure you've seen those already. Tura doesn't want to admit why moving was as easy as it was." He opened the book and held it out to her. "She's worried you'll be upset with us. Abby, we've had the house here for a long time. We only moved into the apartment complex because I had responsibilities there."

"I don't understand." The old newspaper clippings inside the book didn't seem to have any relation to the conversation until she spotted names she recognized. "What the…." She turned the pages. Her parents' wedding announcement, her birth announcement, her grandfather's obituary. A copy of her baptism documentation that listed her grandmother as her godmother… and Wendel Samson as her godfather. The book fell out of her hands.

Wendel grabbed it before it could hit the floor. He smiled sadly, then turned the page and held it back out to her. "We moved into town because of you. I take my promises seriously. Runs in the family, I guess. So we just rented this place out until we needed it again."

"Way to shock her, Buzzard." Dominic pressed against her side, then propped himself on her knee to look at the book himself. "Still, can't fault his attention to detail."

She stared at the black and white photo of the charred remains of her parents' trailer that had apparently graced the front page of the local paper. The accompanying story told about the electrical fire that had started from some chewed cords. It concluded with the fact that the deceased couple's daughter was now in the care of her mother's aunt and uncle.

"I don't have to believe the..." Wendel caught himself. "Anyway, I know Nicky didn't want you buried in the type of crap Davidson spits out. I couldn't do as much as I wanted to, but..." He sighed and turned away to put the book back. "I did what I could."

Abby didn't know what to say. Didn't know what to think. Her entire world had just spun around and turned upside down. The only reason Marlon's family had moved in next door was because of her? She put her head in her hands, forcing Dominic back to the floor. "Marlon always says you have the world wired."

Wendel laughed. "Kid exaggerates. I know how to pull strings like Mom does, but that doesn't mean I manipulate people like a chess game." He reached out and lifted her chin. "What's between you and my son, that's on you two." He ruffled her hair. "I didn't see that one coming."

She shifted uncomfortably, her hand going to the cross Marlon had given her. "I wondered why Aunt Gladys didn't like you."

"Doubt she ever put two and two together honestly. According to Gail, she insisted you be baptized again anyway."

Abby shuddered. She remembered that; she'd argued against it almost as hard as she had that Dominic was real. It wasn't until Gladys had told her if she didn't do it she'd never see her parents again that she had given in. "She did." She hesitated then reached out and squeezed his hand. "I don't know what to say. Thank you." She smiled. "I think I would have gone crazy without you all."

"No need. You kept us sane too," he said. "Still, glad we don't have to keep up appearances anymore." Wendel waved a hand towards the door. "I'm sure you need a moment."

"I would say you do," came Aeneas' voice as she took the offered escape. "Considering he sprang that on you out of the blue clear sky."

Abby just shook her head. *I suppose he could have told me sooner, but...* She sighed. *I would have thrown it at Aunt Gladys pretty fast, and you know what would happened then.*

"Everything happens for a reason," commented Dominic with a smirk. "Isn't that one thing all religions agree on? Even if they don't agree on the why."

"Modern religions have lost more knowledge than they have retained."

She ignored the pair and went looking for Marlon. She found him in the garage working on his motorcycle with his uncle Richie. Marlon had pulled off his goal of getting his motorcycle license last year. Not wanting to disturb them, Abby paused at the door.

"If you're gonna build a swap meet special," Richie told him, shaking his head, "then you need to keep up with it or you'll end up screwed when there's no one else around."

That rung a bell. "Swap meet special?" she repeated. She smiled sheepishly when both turned to look at her. "Sorry, just feel like I've heard that term before."

Marlon rolled his eyes. "It's a song Grandpa likes from an old record he has. I wouldn't be surprised if The Dragon had a copy, too. Just means a bike put together on your own."

Abby joined them. "I thought your bike was a sportster?" She gently brushed Marlon's bangs out of his eyes. "You're jack of all trades, Mars-Bars."

"Like father, like son," said Richie, smiling.

"It is a sportster," Marlon said. He gave her that grin. "Could I talk you into going for a ride with me? Now that you don't have to worry about Mrs. Lynde throwing a fit?"

"When the Destroyer admits he was wrong!" Abby was surprised at the venom in Aeneas's voice. "He wants to risk his life, fine, but you are not –"

"Not what?" countered Dominic with a growl. "I rode for years!"

"And look where it got you!"

"You keep saying that." Dominic's growling got louder. "You keep saying that like it explains everything and you know damn well it doesn't!"

"Never mind, Abs," said Marlon, his face falling at whatever expression he saw on her face. "It was just a thought." He returned his attention to the bike. "Forget it."

Abby ignored the argument between her grandpa's ghost and the angel, focusing instead on what she could do something about. "I never really thought about it," she said, reaching out and touching Marlon's shoulder to get him to look at her. "But I can try." She smiled at the hope in his eyes. "Just don't be upset if I freak out. Remember what I was like learning to drive?"

"You get a death grip on me, beautiful, and you won't hear me complaining." Marlon's smile could have lit up a billboard. "I didn't mean today, though, since school, work…" He trailed off thoughtfully. He reached up and brushed her hair out of her face much as she had his bangs earlier. "This weekend maybe?"

"Those puppy eyes run in the family, too." Before she finished speaking, she had to hold back a wince when Aeneas made another remark. *You're my guardian, not my parent! she mentally snapped at him.* To Marlon she said, "Sure, Mars-"

"Unca Daddy! Unca Daddy SAVE ME!" Isaac burst into the garage. He scrambled up Richie's back and crouched on his shoulders. "Save me!"

"You get back here, you little crap!" Kenny was right behind him. "Uncle Daddy's not gonna save you!" He skidded to a stop when he spotted Abby and Marlon. "Uh, don't mind me. Just in the middle of fratricide." He glared up at Isaac. "I'll make it quick."

"Hey, I didn't get to strangle you," Marlon pointed out, mock-pouting, "so you don't get to strangle him."

"Right now, I wish you had."

Richie sighed. He reached up and pulled Isaac down. He put one hand on his shoulder to keep the little boy from climbing back up. "You're brothers." He locked eyes with each of his nephews one by one. "You should have each other's backs, not be at each other's throats."

"Pretty sure it was that way even in the bible, Uncle Richie," said Marlon with a smirk. "The first murder was between brothers."

"Your dad catches you repeating that recited spiel around your brothers, and you'll be seeing stars, not the light." Richie rubbed his forehead, then nudged Isaac and Kenny out of the garage. "I swear every time you come back from that nuthouse, you sound like – OW!"

"Oops, sorry." Marlon moved his foot off his uncle's as he stood up. "Come on, Abs, let's go see what Felice and Nina are up to."

Abby dipped a curtsy to Richie and followed Marlon out the door. *That was weird.*

"Not really," said Dominic as he trailed alongside them. "Buzzard didn't like you sounding like a preacher around the Marlon and Felice when you were growing up either."

Valid point. Abby bit her lip, then smiled when Marlon took her hand and laced his fingers with hers. She felt her face heat up as he brushed a quick kiss against her temple. *And yet here we are.*

"Yes," said Dominic with a sigh. "Here you are. The Little Wasp trying to keep up with the Dragonfly."

CHAPTER 12

"You have any pants?"

"Pajamas, why?" Abby tilted her head at Felice's question. Marlon had left the room about ten minutes in to go play referee between his brothers, so it was just her and the girls.

Felice put her hands on her hips and clicked her tongue. "Abby, Abby, Abby. You don't think you're actually going to get on a motorcycle in a dress, do you?"

When Abby just looked blank, Felice shook her head.

"Seriously, girl. You'll either end up flashing everyone or catching yourself on fire. We're gonna have to take you shopping."

"Maybe we should take her to one of Grandma's shops?" Nina, Marlon's elder half-sister, set her scrapbook aside. She started sorting the pictures on her desk. "I'm sure they'd have something modest enough."

"I can find some jeans at the thrift store." Abby found herself playing with her cross again. "I mean it's not that big a deal. Marlon wears jeans all the time."

Nina looked offended. "Abby, you're one of us. You can't be caught in thrift store clothes!"

"What do you think I'm wearing right now?" Abby fought not to laugh at the shocked look on the older girl's face. "Sorry, but Aunt Gladys…"

"Was a cheapskate," said Felice. "Plain and simple. I thought you'd gotten some slacks at least now that you don't have to dress

62

like you live at Green Gables. Well, you're going shopping with us tomorrow. End of story. You can come willingly or I'll –"

Abby put her hands up. "I surrender but not tomorrow, Felice. I work, remember?"

Felice's smile would have been scary had Abby not known her so well. "Day after, then. We'll just have to convince brother dear to share."

Nina giggled. "That should be easy enough. If he says no, he can come, too."

Abby's face felt like she could cook an egg on it. She had gone shopping with Felice once. When Melissa needed a prom dress, she had asked them to come along and help her find something "classy yet proper." Felice had made Melissa model everything they picked out like she was on the runway. The idea of doing that... in pants... in front of Marlon... *Mother Mary, pray for me.*

Dominic chuckled. "I'd almost pay to see that."

"You're terrible, I swear." Abby wasn't sure if by that she meant her grandfather, her friends, or both. "OK, Tuesday it is, but don't expect me to do tight fittin' jeans."

"You Catholic girls start much too late," said Felice with a sigh. "Abby, come on, you're eighteen. Live a little."

"I have a life," Abby said as she toyed with the cross. Her fingers rubbed over the spine of the dragon curled around it. "Contrary to popular opinion."

"Come on, Abby, let's see already!"

"I wouldn't wear these in public if Satan took up ice skating!" Abby stared at the dressing room mirror, cringing. "I told you, I'm not doing Conway Twitty!"

Felice's groan said it all. "Abigail Palmer, get your butt out here! Sheesh, this is like trying to bathe a cat!"

"Bathing a cat is easier," Marlon said. "Abs, geez, it can't look that bad."

"You stay out of this Mars-Bars!" Abby swallowed hard. She used her make up mirror to see how they looked from behind and felt her face burn. The problem wasn't that they looked bad. It was that they looked good. Too good.

"The word you're looking for is *normal*," said Dominic from his place on the floor. He had closed his eyes while she changed but was now staring at her like she was dense. "Actually, you look like Nicole did at your age. Go out there and give Little Wasp a heart attack already."

"Is she always this stubborn?" asked Nina.

With a sigh, Abby spun around and exited the dressing room, eyes closed tight so as not to see her boyfriend's face. "I am not dressing like this, Felice. I mean it."

"Turn around," replied Felice, completely unfazed. "I don't see the problem," she added once Abby had obliged. "Do you, sis?"

"Not really. She looks pretty hot."

"Marlon?" Abby braced herself for it to be unanimous. "Your thoughts?"

"Can I plead the fifth?" he said, which got her to open her eyes. He looked like a kid that got caught with a handful of candy right before dinner. "But I'm all for you not wearing 'em in public. I don't want to go to jail."

Nina snorted. "Be serious."

"I am," Marlon replied, rolling his eyes. "Some idiot will open his mouth, I'll hit him, and end up behind bars for assault." He picked up the pair she'd picked out herself and tossed them to her. "Here, Abs, let's give your choice a try."

She grabbed them like a lifeline and disappeared back into the dressing room. She switched as fast as she could, then dared to check her reflection. The soft fabric didn't feel glued to her skin at least, or look painted on. A smile crossed her face. She walked back out and spun around. "Now, this I can live with."

"Much better." Marlon grinned. "Ding ding! We have a winner."

Felice facepalmed. "Oh hush. You're just saying that because it's her pick. Abby, seriously? You'll need a belt to keep those from falling off."

Abby didn't see the problem. "If they were *that* loose, they would have already." They were just loose enough they didn't hug her frame. "They're comfortable."

"So, I'm being supportive." Marlon started folding up the rejects. "What's wrong with that?"

"Leashed, collared, and panting," said Dominic, shaking his head. "Just like his grandfather."

Felice looked from her brother to Abby and sighed. "Fine, fine. At least it's a step in the right direction. I'm still surprised we found anything decent in a thrift store."

Abby went back into the dressing room to put her skirt back on. She folded the jeans over her arm and rejoined the Samsons. "Compromises, Felice." She smiled. "Still, thank you."

"Thank me when you realize how much more comfortable pants are."

That evening Abby, clad in her pajamas, turned on the laptop. She didn't make it two minutes before her messenger window popped open. To her surprise, it wasn't Marlon, but a friend she'd made on the forum.

RaspberryRaposa: Hope you didn't plan to write a book or something based on our RPs, Dfly. They're all gone.

DragonflyGirl: What?

RaspberryRaposa: I dunno, I just went to log in and got a "This forum has been deleted." message.

Abby clicked the shortcut and sure enough:

WE'RE SORRY. THIS FORUM HAS BEEN DELETED DUE TO NONCOMPLIANCE WITH THE SITE GUIDELINES. WE APOLOGIZE FOR ANY INCONVENIENCE.

Returning to the messenger, Abby typed, "Noncompliance with site guidelines"?

RaspberryRaposa: The Queens have been messing with the site's source code for a while now. You aren't SUPPOSED TO, but no one actually checks it. Though if it gets reported they act pretty darn swift.

DragonflyGirl: So that means…

RaspberryRaposa: Someone reported it just to get it shut down. Did I miss something this week or what? I mean, why would anyone do this?

DragonflyGirl: Only thing I can think of is Jenner got into it with GreenQueen on Saturday. Random spends more time on there than I do though, he might know if anything else went down.

RaspberryRaposa: I'll check with him then. Dang it, now what are we supposed to do?

Abby felt helpless as she typed, "We'll think of something."

RaspberryRaposa: I hope you're right, Dfly. Would suck to lose friends over a damn game.

DragonflyGirl: I gotta agree with you there.

That wasn't the last conversation she had on the subject either. WaterHorse, PlumFelidae, and in short, every friend she'd made, contacted her wanting to know if she knew anything. No one was sure who had reported the site, but suspicion was flying around like bats in a belfry. The top suspects were Drew and GreenQueen, but really it could have been anyone. The Queens had kicked quite a few members over the years.

DragonflyGirl: I'd love to play Sherlock some more, but I need some sleep.

Abby copied and pasted the message to each of her friends, then smiled as one by one they wished her goodnight. She shut off the computer and got into bed. Wrapped in her blankets, her kitten curled up under her chin, she was soon dreaming.

CHAPTER 13

She clung to Marlon, resting her cheek against his back as she kept her eyes tightly closed. Her heart was hammering in her chest. Her hair whipped behind her. All she could think was "too fast." She tried to ask him to slow down, but the roar of the bike drowned out her voice. If she could just get his attention, she knew he'd listen. He always listened. Always. She screamed his name as they rounded a corner and a bright light struck her closed eyes.

Abby groaned as the blaring of her alarm clock broke through. She glared at the window then down at the kitten tangled in the fallen curtain. She had an hour before she had to be downstairs for work. Thankfully she had had no homework today, hence why she risked the nap. "Dommy, you have got to stop playing in the curtains."

"I don't," said Dominic, chuckling.

"Very funny." Abby picked up her kitten and locked him in his crate so she could put the curtains back up. She grabbed her desk chair to use as a stool. "And, Aeneas, if that dream was your idea of a joke, it was a pretty poor one."

"Manipulating your dreams is unnecessary as you can hear me quite clearly," replied the angel. "Getting you to listen is another matter entirely."

"Marlon wouldn't put me in danger," she countered. She started to step off her desk chair. "He loves me. Too much sometimes, but he loves me." Just as her foot touched the floor, the chair was jerked out from under her and she tumbled backwards. She slammed on the floor, and pain shot through her back and her rear. She pushed up on one elbow to see the chair spin around on its own and land backwards across from her. She pulled herself into a sitting position and clapped sarcastically. "What's next? You'll pull a rabbit out of your hat?"

Dominic moved beside her and growled loudly. "Long time no see, Wormwood."

"You immature –!" Aeneas' voice was louder than The Dragon's growls.

"Whoa, tough crowd." Bjarte appeared, sitting in the chair, his arms crossed over the back with his chin resting upon them. "Miss me?"

Abby got up, walked over, and jerked the chair away from him. She returned it to her desk. "Isn't there a well-placed uncle in the Lowerarchy you could be writing?"

"When it comes to advice, I'd be the one givin' it out, not askin' for it." Bjarte leaned against the wall with a grin. "Annie, help me out here? When she falls, will that make a hundred or a hundred and one I've beat you to?"

"She is not going to fall, so the point is moot."

"I don't have time to deal with your mind games," said Abby, getting out her work uniform. She went into the bathroom to change. She closed her eyes as she did so, just in case the demon decided to follow. Once dressed she returned to her bedroom and filled Domino's water dish. "I have to work tonight. So get thee behind me…" She narrowed her eyes. "Screwtape."

"Gladly." His smirk was chilling. "After all, it's a fine view."

Abby clenched her fists and bolted out the door.

"Hey! Sweetmeats! Can we get another round over here?"

"I can't serve alcohol, sir, I'm under age." Abby flinched when the customer replied and called her a name she was sure even Bryan wouldn't have used. The customer questioned her vision and pointed out that they lacked a certain part of the male anatomy. "I'm sorry, it's kinda dark in here." *I sure hope Sam's just trying to save on the electric bill,* thought Abby. *Otherwise this is ridiculous.*

During the day, the windows let in enough light to navigate the uneven floor. After dark the bar could have been a horror film setting. She supposed that was why only the lunch crowd sometimes included families. If any child saw this, they would have nightmares for a month.

"I'll find someone who can get your order, ma'am." Abby tried to signal one of the other girls. She knew most of her fellow employees by sight if not by name. She finally understood Sam's comments about strays. It seemed everyone that worked there had had a hard start. Two sisters referred to Bryan as "uncle". From what she could see, there might have been no blood between them, but they were still family.

The angry customer got up and grabbed Abby's arm. "Look you - " That word again. Did these people have a vocabulary at all? "Do I look like a dried up –?"

"Hands off." Sam appeared at Abby's shoulder, wiping his hands with the rag that always seemed to be in his grip. "My staff ain't playthings."

The customer obliged and returned to her chair. She curled her lip at him and crudely asked if he could take her order. "Why you got jailbait workin' here anyway? Ain't that bad for business?"

"I'll deal with this, Dragonfly." Sam gestured with his rag for her to get moving. He pulled a pad out of his apron pocket along with a pen. "No one here's under eighteen. Just not all of 'em are drinkin' age. Tell me what you're after and I'll see if we got it."

That's the creepiest one yet, she thought as she dodged patrons and fellow wait staff through the dimly lit bar. *Almost as creepy as -*

"Nice broad," came Bjarte's voice. "Bet you could have had a real good time. Since ya obviously ain't jumped Prince Charmin' yet. Oh wait, forgot ya don't swing that way. Shame."

Abby refused to respond. She busied herself clearing a table after its occupants stumbled out the door, carefully stacking the glasses on her tray.

"You know, Wormwood… there's this thing called a succubus," said Dominic as he leapt up into the recently vacated booth. "Maybe you should look one up. Much as you talk about it, seems you're the one that needs to get laid."

The demon didn't get the chance to respond. As she lifted the tray, Abby felt a hand squeeze her rear. She turned and struck the offender with the tray, tossing the glasses to the floor where they shattered like ice. A loud string of cussing from the offender followed.

"Whoa, broad's got a mouth on her don't she?" Bjarte's laughter rang in her ears. "I think she might feel you over-reacted, Abs."

Abby stared. *I can't believe she tried that after Sam just told her off.* Then she noticed the foul-mouthed woman was clutching her face. For the second time in her life Abby had given someone a bloody nose.

"And it was just as justified this time," Dominic moved in front of her, a low growl rumbling in his throat. "Sam already set her straight. He won't put up with this either."

Right on cue, Sam appeared and grabbed the back of the woman's shirt. All around them everyone froze to watch. Sam half-dragged, half-pushed her across the room.

The customer struggled against his hold, but was unable to break free as one hand covered her nose in an effort to stanch the blood that already covered the lower half of her face.

"Next time, read the sign!" Sam shoved her out the door and slammed it behind her. In response to her crude gestures through the window, he pointed up the neon sign in the corner that clearly stated waitresses were not responsible if patrons crossed the line. Disgust written all over his face, Sam turned to the crowd. "What are you all lookin' at? Ain't you ever seen a man do his job before?"

Everyone rushed to go back to their own business, from the customers to the staff. Feeling her face flush, Abby knelt and started to use the tray to gather up the shards. *I... I didn't mean to...* Back when she'd hit Drew, there had been anger, indignation. This had been nothing but shock.

"Leave it." She looked up to the voice and saw Sam with the broom and dustpan. "Clock out, Dragonfly. You got school tomorrow."

She wanted to protest, but the words couldn't get past the lump in her throat. She just nodded, put the tray on the table and headed for the back door.

"You were justified, Abigail." Aeneas's voice followed her up the stairs to her room. "You have no reason for guilt."

"Oh really? I shouldn't feel bad I broke a stranger's nose?" Abby slammed the bathroom door behind her. She quickly took off her uniform and changed into pajamas. "I shouldn't feel bad I destroyed I don't know how many glasses? That I made a mess I didn't even get the chance to clean up?" She threw the door open and flinched when it bounced off the wall. "That I didn't even try to argue? That I just did as I was told like a five-year-old?"

"You're acting like a five-year-old now," said Dominic. "You defended yourself, end of story. Calm down, young lady. You're making a fool of yourself."

Before she could say a word, her cell phone rang. Abby looked to where was charging on her nightstand. Wendel had given the phone to her some time ago, but she hadn't even used it. She could only think of one reason it would be ringing now.

"Better answer it, Abs." Bjarte appeared, leaning against the wall beside the nightstand. "Or you'll have your monkey climbin' in your window again." His grin just added fuel to the fire. "Then again, maybe you'd like that."

"GO TO HELL!" Abby rushed over and snatched the phone off the table. It jerked free from the cord as she snapped it open. "WHAT?"

There was a sharp intake of breath on the other end of the line. "Uh, um, you OK Abs?"

"Marlon." Abby fought to keep her voice at a normal volume. "I'm *fine*, thank you. Why are you calling this late?" She braced herself to hear her suspicions confirmed. To hear her every move was being watched. Because of course she couldn't take care of herself. Of course she needed someone to rush in and save her before things went too far.

"Just... just wanted to know if you were still up for riding this weekend?" His voice was cracking somewhat. "If you didn't pick up I'd have left a message."

"So..." She sat on the bed, thrusting a pillow to her chest to give herself something to do with her free hand. She was holding it and the phone so tightly her hands were shaking. "This has nothing to do with, say, Sam calling you?"

"Why would he call *me*?"

"I don't know," she said, her voice slowly going up in volume. "Why are you calling to ask me about plans that are three days away when you could damn well ask me at school tomorrow?" She didn't give him the chance to respond. "When you've never called me, ever? If you want to get ahold of me, you use the messenger. You told me to message you the first night, remember? It was your dad who said to call. So I don't know, Marlon, you tell me!"

Marlon mentally swore. Truthfully, no one had called him. Sam had called his father. He had simply overheard enough to worry him. So he had called her. He needed to hear her voice, just to be sure she was all right. Now he was stuck in the hole he had dug with no idea how to get out. "Abs... I just, I worry about you OK?" He started talking faster, trying to get the words out before she could get angrier. "I know you can take care of yourself, I just... you've..."

"I've what?" she demanded. "Just 'cause I'm no longer under my great-aunt's thumb doesn't mean I'm made of glass, Marlon! I've dealt with worse than some pushy b –!"

"I KNOW THAT!" he protested. *I've really done it now.* "I know you've... you're... Abs you've been through Hell and survived. Excuse me for trying to keep you from going back!"

Her sigh cut him. "Marlon," she said, her voice at least calm again. "I appreciate the thought, but this isn't a fairy tale, OK? You can't lock me in a tower and protect me from everything."

"Yeah," he replied, forcing a chuckle. "That would be kidnapping and I'd end up in jail."

"Mars-Bars." He could almost see her shaking her head. There was a smile in her voice again at least. "I trust you. I need you to trust me. If I need help, I'll ask, I promise. Just.... You realize you're coming off like one of those Prince-Charming-slash-stalker-romance heroes right?"

"WHAT?" he choked. "I am not!"

She laughed. "Well, let's see. So far you've climbed in my window while I was asleep, you've obviously got me being babysat or you wouldn't have called tonight... want me to go on?"

"I don't have people babysitting you, Abs." He rolled his eyes. "Sam called Dad so he'd hear it from him first instead of through the grapevine, and I overheard them talking. That's all." When she didn't reply, he started fidgeting. "Abs? I'm sorry, but I'm a Samson.

74

Grandpa worries about Grandma, Dad worries about Mom, and I worry about you. Blame my bloodline."

"I worry about you, too, Mars-Bars. But I don't go rushing to your rescue."

He sighed. "You punched Drew for being an idiot once."

"That's different. OK, OK, valid point, but just… try and tone it down? Look, we can talk about it tomorrow. I need to get to sleep and so do you. Goodnight, Mars-Bars. I love you. I want to strangle you sometimes, but I love you."

He chuckled again. "Back at ya, Abs." He realized what he'd said and sputtered. "I-I mean I love you, too! Not the strangling part! OK you know what? I'm gonna get off here before I put my foot so far in my mouth it comes out the other end. Goodnight, Abs. Sweet dreams." He waited until she returned the sentiment and hung up before closing his phone. He flopped back onto his bed. He ran the conversation over and over in his head until he finally fell asleep.

CHAPTER 14

"OK, son, spill. What's eating you?"

Marlon tried pretending to be too busy eating his breakfast to hear her. When his mother kept staring at him, waiting, he sighed. "Nothing, Mom. I'm at the top of the food chain." She bought that line as much as he did whenever Abby tried it on him. He finally confessed the whole conversation, which was now burned into his memory. Thankfully, his siblings were too caught up in their own business at the breakfast table to pay attention.

His mother cupped his chin with a knowing smile. "You are your father's son. When a Samson finds his 'lady,' the first instinct is to shelter and protect his delicate, fragile creature."

His father rolled his eyes. "The only problem is we tend to pick partners that are neither."

"So you adjust," said his uncle Richie with a cocky grin. "You still run interference." He leaned close and whispered, "You just get sneakier about it."

"And face the music when you get caught." Wendel caught his brother in a headlock and gave him a quick noogie before letting go.

"Buzzard Breath!" Richie reached up and fought to fix his hair. "We're not kids anymore."

"It was either that or slap you, and I'd aim low if I slapped."

Richie's face turned bright red. He faceplamed. "Shoulda saw that coming."

Datura shook her head indulgently at the brothers before turning back to Marlon. "I'm sure Abby won't hold it against you. But your timing was... pretty bad."

"I don't see what I did wrong." Marlon put his head in his hands. "I know she can take care of herself. But before..."

"Before you were right next door if she needed back up," Wendel finished. "We all were."

Richie picked at his plate. "Well, you kinda did rush to her rescue recently, instead of waiting to see if she had a solution herself. She likely thought this was more of the same."

Marlon tilted his head in confusion. "I haven't done anything I didn't before. I brought her breakfast. The window thing was 'cause she mentioned it." He cringed at the memory. "I should have thought that one through a bit more, but still, same old same old."

His parents and uncle shared a look, then Richie smirked. "So you routinely found her a place to live and a job to go with it? Man, I must have really been out of it."

Marlon felt the blood rush to his face. "I didn't do that, Dad and Grandpa did."

"You called me, knowing I'd find a way to fix it. You set the wheels in motion." Wendel reached over without looking and broke up Kenny and Isaac's squabble. "Enough you two! Manners at the table." He returned to the subject at hand. "Pretty sure she sees it that way, too."

"Great, so I'm in the doghouse for caring?" He slumped in his chair. "Wonderful."

"They say all's fair in love and war," his father said. "The truth is, nothing's fair in either."

Felice picked up the dishes and put them in the sink. "We better get moving, bro. Don't want to be late for school."

Marlon just nodded and followed. "Thanks," he said to his parents, then bolted out the door.

Felice got on her bicycle, then paused when she caught his expression. "You OK, bro?"

"Yeah, just got a lot on my mind," he replied. "See you at school." Once she was out of sight, he considered his options. Any other day, he would have gotten in the car he shared with his siblings and picked his lady up. *But after last night, it'd be like walking into a minefield.* He got his own bike out and started after his sister. *"Tone it down," huh? Well, let's start here.* He shook his head and sighed. *Who am I kidding?* He didn't really blame her. *I'm just not up to another talk about how I screwed up.* Besides, after his parents' advice he was pretty sure he'd reached his quota of awkward conversations for the day.

Hopefully seeing him take her words to heart would keep her from bringing it up at all.

The best laid plans always screw up. Marlon fidgeted where he stood, leaning beside the front doors at school. Class started in five minutes. Abby was late, and he was so close to pacing it wasn't funny. The worst part was the worry was his own dang fault. *Could have just gone and picked her up, but nooo. I had to be a stupid coward!* His hand brushed against the phone in his pocket before going to the cross she'd given him around his neck. *Please, let her be OK.* Just as he had made up his mind that the tongue-lashing would be worth it, he saw her car pull in. *Thank you, God.* He started to walk over to her, but froze when Abby slammed her door and he heard voices call out to her.

"Heard you got a nice swing, Palmer!"

"You go girl! Way to teach that dyke a lesson!"

"My brother actually asked if I had your number, you believe that?"

Marlon clenched his teeth and his hands, struggling to control the fury that coursed through him. She wouldn't welcome the defense, and acting on his impulses would get him expelled. He forced himself to lean back against the wall, folding his arms across his chest as he waited.

As she walked, Abby glared at the catcallers. When she saw him, an expression of guilt washed over her pretty face.

Much as he wanted to cross the distance and kiss it away, he held himself in place. Still, he gave her a smile. "Good morning, beautiful."

"Morning, Mars-Bars." Abby smiled slightly and sighed. "I'm sorry I overreacted last night. I was just..." She flinched and threw a glare over her shoulder at yet another idiot before returning her attention to him. "Stressed and you got the brunt of it. I shouldn't have blasted you."

Oh, now she's apologizing? Wasn't too upset, or she'd have called to see where you were when you weren't where you were supposed to be. Marlon caught his anger fighting for an outlet and leashed it. She knew him well enough to check at school first. *She was probably late 'cause she was waiting to see if I'd show.* "Abs, can we just drop it, please? I already got an earful from my parents this morning. Mind if I walk you to class?"

"Of course not." Abby flicked her gaze to his shaking white-knuckled hands.

Marlon pushed off the wall and sighed when she quickly took one of his hands in hers. He rubbed his thumb over the back of her hand, smiling slightly at the way she gripped his in return. Reassuringly. Knowingly. Out of habit he opened the door for her and followed her inside.

Why can't they just shut up? Abby bit back a groan as the catcalls and

79

praise followed them down the hall. It was unbelievable how many students apparently had family that were patrons at Sam's bar. She glanced down at Marlon's white-knuckled hand. *I wonder which of us will snap first. It's bugging him as much as me.*

"Wonder why Prince Charming's so … frustrated." Bjarte's voice rang in her ears, laced with laughter. "His street cred has to be through the roof, since everyone's gotta believe he's tapping what ya wouldn't let her play with."

"You know what they say about assuming," said Dominic with a low growl. "Little Wasp has more respect for his lady than half these clowns would theirs."

And that's the gospel truth! Abby clenched her teeth as she walked alongside her boyfriend to her homeroom class. When they stopped outside the door, she took a deep breath.

Marlon pulled his hand free off hers, then shoved both his hands in his pockets. He started to smile, then glared over her head. "Don't let the idiots get to you." He leaned over and kissed her forehead. "Check ya later."

Once more she mentally kicked herself for her outburst the night before. "Later, Mars-Bars." She hurried to her desk, eager for class to start and shut down the gossip.

"Working hard or hardly working?" Melissa sat down at the desk beside her. She propped her chin up with one hand and smiled. "If rumors are true, you're settling in to your new life nicely."

"I plead the Fifth." Abby fought back a groan. She sighed in relief as the teacher came in and all conversation silenced.

"So…" Abby said as they all sat down for lunch, bracing herself for the answer. "How's life for Preacher Davidson's flock?"

Melissa knew what she was really asking. "Dolores has been keeping Gladys busy. Both stopped demanding status reports." She kept her eyes on her food. "Though occasionally they ask... sorta indirectly... some pretty stupid questions. Knowing you, after all, and it hasn't even been a month..."

"Something tells me I can guess them." Abby sighed. She laid her hand over Marlon's. He was shaking again. "I don't know why I'm surprised."

Felice glanced at her brother and smiled. "That's adorable." She buttered her toast. "Thinking you waited until you had some privacy to express your love in its purest form."

Marlon looked at his sister like she grew a second head. "Felice, they're talking about Abs like they do *Mom*." He turned his hand over and laced his fingers through Abby's in an obvious attempt to distract himself.

"And the problem with that is?" Felice narrowed her eyes.

Abby knew that look. "I'd rather be compared with your mother, Mars-Bars, than Aunt Gladys." She picked up her sandwich with her free hand and took a bite.

Marlon's eyes softened at that. "Yeah. I can see why." He released Abby's hand with a sheepish expression and turned back to Melissa. "So how's your man?"

Melissa didn't answer for at least a minute, her eyes scanning the room. "Did something happen in that game of yours?"

"Why?"

"Because he's been..." Melissa looked up at her. "Something's been eating at him since Saturday, and since he hasn't told me... it has to be the game. He won't discuss it in front of his parents, and he's been too buried in his schoolwork to go anywhere else to talk."

"He got kicked after killing off his character." Abby held up her hand when asked for more details. "It's a long story, Mel and I'm not even sure I know it all." Abby jerked her thumb at Marlon. "Random here would know more than I do."

Marlon wasted no time giving a rundown of Saturday's events and the mystery of just who reported the forum to shut it down. "Most of them are blaming him, but honestly I wouldn't put it past GreenQueen either."

"He loved that game. It was his escape if nothing else." She ducked her head, tearing up her roll. "And he knew how much it meant to everyone else. I can't see him being as petty as his father." She sighed. "Not that anyone would believe it."

Marlon looked at Abby before nodding. "He's not a *complete* jerk after all. People can get beyond their upbringing."

Abby bit her tongue at the double-meaning in his words. She just wanted him to stop running to her rescue at the drop of a hat, not change his entire personality. *How do I get that across?* She cringed when a few people passed their table to empty their trays, snickering as they tossed out more commentary on her actions the night before.

"Don't they have anything better to do?" Marlon asked through his teeth. He shot a glare at Melissa. "It's not funny!"

Abby rolled her eyes at her friend's tight-lipped laughter. "That's unladylike, Mrs. Davidson."

"Oh, hush, you two." Melissa grinned. "They'll find something else to talk about eventually. Enjoy your fifteen minutes of fame."

"Bro," said Felice. "Take a chill pill. You're acting like Grandpa."

"I am not!"

Abby's free hand went to her cross. "Something else to talk about..." She rubbed the dragon's spine, taking comfort in the familiar shape. She gathered her nerve as an idea occurred to her.

"I would beg you to reconsider." Aeneas sounded resigned. "But I am well aware that would fail miserably."

Oh ye of little faith. Abby braced herself mentally. *Marlon won't let me get hurt after all, and this will at least get them to talk about something I'd be proud of.* She glanced down at The Dragon beside her. *I might actually like it. After all, Grandpa Nick did.*

"That I did," said Dominic with a smile. "There's no freer feeling in the world, though I could name a few more pleasant ones."

Careful, she thought, *or I'll start to think Screwtape's wearing the mask again.* "Marlon?" Abby smiled when he looked up at her. "Can I talk you into picking me up tomorrow?" When his eyes widened so did her grin. "I'm thinking I could try out those jeans a little early." She wanted to laugh at the way his expression lit up.

"You mean it?" Marlon's voice cracked in his excitement. "Hell yeah!" Concern crept back into his eyes. "You sure though?"

"I'm sure," she told him. "One, I trust you. Two..." She leaned over and kissed his cheek. "Let's give them something to talk about."

Melissa looked from one to the other, then at the grinning Felice. "Someone want to tell me what's going on?"

"And spoil the surprise?" Marlon was grinning from ear to ear. "Naw, you can find out along with everyone else."

CHAPTER 15

Abby stared at the stranger in her mirror the next morning. She wore the jeans and a long-sleeve sweater with the black nylon boots she saved for rainy days. Her hair was tied back in a ponytail and the jacket Bryan had given her two years ago was slung over her shoulder. The only thing normal about her outfit were the silver studs in her ears that matched the charm bracelet and the dragon cross. "I look like an idiot."

"For all that, you may be one for even considering this stunt," came Aeneas' voice, "I assure you, you do not look the part."

"Again, the word is *normal*." Dominic shook his head. "And she's not being stupid. Little Wasp will appreciate this, and, if she actually enjoys it, they'll have something to do that's not sitting in front of a screen all day."

"Go ahead, Screwtape," she said to the empty room. "I know you're just dying to toss your two cents in."

"Ya know, I find it funny you can't even say my name." He appeared beside the cat cage, making playful gestures at Domino, then laughed when the kitten backed up and hissed. "You can act like you ain't scared of me all ya want, yet that one little detail speaks volumes."

"Get. Away. From. Him." Abby slung the jacket on as the distant roar of a motorcycle reached them. She had to deal with this before Marlon got there. "You touch him and I swear –"

"Oh relax." Bjarte stood up and crossed his arms. "He's useless to me locked up like that. Now, loose, I could work with." His grin chilled her to the bone. "Amazing how useful small animals can be, ain't it, Annie?"

"You foul, disgusting –!" The rest of the angel's reply was drowned out by Marlon's arrival.

The roar of the bike cut off and they all heard the footsteps on the stairs. Abby narrowed her eyes at the demon. "What are you hinting at this time? Enough of the mind games!"

"Nothing you can do a thing about now." Bjarte's grin just got wider. "Twelve years ago and some change, maybe, but not now."

Dominic growled and stepped between them, his tail lashing from side to side. His anger only confirmed the picture her mind had put together.

Twelve years ago, she had been six years old. Twelve years ago, her parents had died in a fire caused by the cords Troubadour had chewed almost in half. Shock went through her. "No."

"Yeah, you get it now, don't you? If I were you, I'd make sure to keep kitty locked up nice and tight. Else there might be … accidents."

Marlon's knock at the door made her almost jump out of her skin. "I'll be right out!" She turned and glared at the demon. *Aeneas is right. You understand nothing.* With that, she unlocked the door and walked out.

"Good morning, beaut –" Marlon stopped short and blinked. He slowly ran his eyes from her head to her toes. "Whoa."

Abby felt her face heat up. "That bad, huh?"

"What?" Marlon's gaze snapped to hers. "Bad? Hell, no." He shook his head. "Give me a sec here, I need to find a way to phrase this without sounding..." He trailed off as his eyes made the circuit again. He swallowed hard. "Uh, I..." He tilted his head to the side. "Abs, you wear your hair like that, it's gonna be all in your face even with the helmet on. Here." He crossed the distance and moved behind her, then started to braid her ponytail.

The shiver that went through her had little to do with the chill in the air. The feeling of his hands in her hair... *What is wrong with me?* He was finished before she could really pinpoint what she was feeling. She turned around and smiled. "Thank you."

He held out his hand. "Come on Abs." The feeling returned as he took her hand in his and walked her down the stairs. Marlon took her backpack from her and tucked it into one of the saddle bags. He lifted the helmet from the seat, carefully fitted it onto her head then tightened the chin strap. "There we go." He put his own helmet on, then mounted the bike and shot her a grin. "Ready when you are."

"So just... get on?" Abby eyed the bike nervously.

He nodded and pointed out the foot pegs. "Don't worry. You can't hurt the bike any."

She took a deep breath and put one hand on his shoulder, the other on the seat, and swung herself up behind him. "Now what?"

"Wrap your arms around him, silly." Dominic shook his head at her. "And try and keep still, or you'll distract him. Relax, it's not hard."

Marlon gently reached back and moved her hand off his shoulder to around his waist, then pulled the other to rest on top. He looked back and the expression on his face sent warmth all through her body. "Do you trust me?"

"The last time you asked me that, I was on a bike, too, and the answer hasn't changed." She laughed and felt a smile on her lips. "Yes, do you honestly think I would be here if I didn't?"

"Then let's start building some memories." Marlon kick-started the bike and started out onto the street. "And give them something to really talk about."

"Hang on, Dragonfly," said Dominic with a smile as he took wing. "Little Wasp is gonna show you how to soar."

Abby pressed her cheek into Marlon's back and braced herself. Contrary to her expectations, though, he never went much faster than the cars that shared the morning commute with them. She began to relax just as they pulled into the school parking lot.

Marlon parked the bike near the front door, then gently removed her hands. "Wasn't so bad now, was it?" He dismounted then offered his hand to help her down.

"No," she admitted with a smile. "It wasn't. Thank you."

"Anytime, Abs." He removed her helmet then his own and put them away. He ran a hand through his hair. "Want me to get your books until you get your balance back?"

Abby was a little unsteady on her feet, but she shook her head. "I can manage, but thanks anyway." She held out a hand for her bag and slung it over her shoulder. As the catcallers' voices started around them, she reached up and kissed Marlon's cheek.

"Dang, Abs," he said, grinning as he took her hand. "You weren't kidding were you?"

She smiled and laced her hand with his. "Nope. Come on, Mars-Bars, let's get to class."

CHAPTER 16

Abby adjusted little by little over the next week, and saw Felice proven right. Life finally settled into a workable routine, which included a change in her wardrobe and mode of transportation. The calls and stares made her uncomfortable, and sadly brought Marlon's protective side out in full force. But the jeans were far more practical, since Marlon was there each day to pick her up. Riding wasn't so bad, and seeing his eyes light up made it worth it.

"I'll be darned!" Gail laughed out loud when they pulled up on Marlon's bike and parked outside her apartment. She stepped out to greet them. "Look at you two! Chips off the old blocks."

Abby swung down to the sidewalk and tilted her head. She jerked a thumb at Marlon. "I get it on his end, but me?"

Gail just smiled. "You look just like your mother out with your father."

"Biggest difference is Little Wasp actually knows how to ride." Dominic sighed. "He could have given Cowboy a few lessons."

"Explains why you caught on so quick, Abs." Marlon removed her helmet then his own. "Runs in the family."

"Yes," came Aeneas' commentary. "Foolish choices certainly do."

Oh will you lighten up already? Abby dug into the saddlebag for the package they had brought. *I don't know who's more annoying, you or Screwtape.* She walked over and hugged her grandmother. "Happy birthday, Grandma." She held out the box.

"Thank you, dear. It's so good to see you." Gail took the box, then looked up at Marlon and smiled. "Both of you. Ready to lose, Little Wasp?"

Marlon shoved his hands in his pockets and flashed a grin. "Ma'am, I think I can give you a run for your mints this time. I've been practicing."

"Come on and get out of the cold," she replied, ushering them inside. "I swear that swagger skipped a generation."

"Not sure about that, ma'am." Marlon took off his boots and set them by the door. "Dad and Uncle Richie have their moments, too."

Abby followed suit, then headed into the kitchen to get drinks, leaving her boyfriend and grandmother to talk. Just as she got the glasses down she heard Gail's voice behind her.

"You just go ahead and deal, young man, I'll be right with you." Gail walked into the kitchen and gave her a smile. "You're looking well, Abby." She scanned her outfit. "Though I never would have expected to see you in jeans if I lived to be a hundred."

"You can't ride a motorcycle in a dress apparently," she replied. A small smile curled her lips. "Besides, I trip less at the bar." She froze when Gail laid a hand on hers.

"You know that boy's serious, don't you?" Gail said, her pitch lowered so as not to carry.

Abby pulled away. She went to the fridge and got the lemonade out. "Mars-Bars?" she replied, filling the glasses. She returned the pitcher to the fridge and looked for a tray. "You're kidding, right?"

"Don't be dense Abigail," said Dominic. "It doesn't suit you."

Gail put her hands on her hips and her expression matched her late husband's tone. "Little Wasp is as see-through as his grandfather. He's thinking long-term, and frankly, dear if you're not..."

"Grandma," she said, turning to meet the older woman's eyes. She dropped her voice to match the whisper. "Are you really going to tell me if I don't hear wedding bells in the future with Mars-Bars...?" Her eyes narrowed. "Please don't start channeling Aunt Gladys."

"Excuse you?" Dominic sat beside her and nipped her leg.

His widow was just as offended. "Abigail Dominique Palmer." She crossed her arms across her chest. "I am *not* my sister, and I will thank you to not compare us. I just know one thing: You don't lead a Samson on. It doesn't end well."

"I'm not." Abby sighed and looked toward the living room. "But how do you know he's... I mean, first Sam, now you. He's acting like every other boy 'in love' I've ever heard of."

Gail gave her a knowing smile. "I've watched both Wasp and

Buzzard with their 'ladies,'" she replied. "There's... tells if you will, and Little Wasp has all of them."

Dominic smiled. "Saw that for a long while now."

Then why didn't you tell me? Abby started at her grandmother, stunned. "I..." She didn't know what to say.

"I didn't think you needed me to tell you," replied The Dragon with a shrug. "After all, a guy doesn't just rush to a woman's aid like he does yours unless he's got it bad."

Marlon wandered around the small living room while he waited. He assumed that Gail was taking a moment to get a rundown of how Abby was doing in private. At least that's what he kept telling himself. Because if the conversation was over *him* and the... risks he was taking with her... His eyes fell on the old photo of his grandfather and The Dragon. *I wonder what you'd have to say about all of this, old man?* He thought over the concepts he'd drawn up for the game he had yet to show Abby. *Would you say I was overstepping or laugh your head off like Grandpa does at the twist of fate?*

Sometimes his brother teased him about picking a girl without a living patriarch around. He didn't have an overprotective father or grandfather to deal with. Just his own doubts either would think him good enough for her. He knew more about The Dragon, Abby's grandfather, than Cowboy though, so that was where his mind went most of the time. That and he knew Nick Whelan's favor was the one that would have counted with his own patriarchs. His gaze moved among the photographs, noticing his father and his father's siblings among some of them, alongside the young woman he knew was Abby's mother. Mixed in though, were the ones his mother had taken of Abby with him and his siblings. The echoes between them were unsettling.

Maybe your father is so accepting because he's living through you? He tried to shake the thought aside. His father loved his mother... and his uncle, though that often went unspoken. *And looks like once upon a time he and "Nicky" were pretty close...* No. If his father had had a crush on The Dragon's daughter, he would have already said as much by now.

"What are you standing around for?" Gail's voice made him jump. Her smile made him feel guilty. "Come sit down... so I can wipe the floor with you."

Abby walked past him and sat the tray on the table in the middle of the hands he'd dealt. She placed a glass beside each and left the tray in place as she sat down.

"Ma'am, no offense, but card shark you may be," he said, trying to sound more confident than he felt. "There's no game I can't master in time."

"Except Path of the Dragon," said Abby with a smile. "I believe that's the only stain on your pristine record, Mars-Bars."

Gail sat down and picked up her cards. "How is that going, by the way?"

Marlon looked at Abby sheepishly. "Uh, well, been drawing some concept art but... as to getting it out there..."

"Haven't had time to try, Grandma." Abby sipped her drink and shifted her cards. "I'll look up more on that when I get home." She smiled for a moment. "I'm finally adjusting. It's... life's nice."

"That's good to hear." Gail dropped a handful of peppermints on the tray. "Well, place your bets, children. And let's have ourselves a card game."

Marlon dropped two candy bars on top of Abby's packs of gum. He shot his lady a grin. "When I play," he said, looking at his hand, "I play for keeps."

Abby returned the smile then quickly looked away, her free hand going to her cross in a dead giveaway. Something was wrong. Again.

How am I gonna get it out of her this time? Marlon sighed. He knew his reaction to the fools at school was grating on her nerves, but he couldn't quite curb the fury. She was *his*. A tiny voice in the back of his mind whispered, *Only if she wants to be.*

CHAPTER 17

"Why so serious, Dragonfly?"

"Don't call me that." Abby refused to look at the demon where he leaned against her desk. She kept her eyes on the search results as she tried to find out more about game distribution. "My name is Abigail. Abby. *Not* 'Abs' or 'Dragonfly'. Those names are reserved."

"You don't use mine, so why should I use yours?" He laughed. "You do realize fear of the name only increases fear of the thing itself?"

"I guess that means you're afraid of me?" She scrolled on, hoping for something she could actually understand. All she saw were games that were already out, or advice not to approach the big name companies. *Why is this so hard?*

Suddenly the air in the room went ice cold. The hair stood up on her arms and the back of her neck. Every nerve went on edge as a feeling of danger took over. She just managed to pull her hands away from the laptop before the lid was slammed shut.

"In your dreams, Abigail. In. Your. Dreams."

The chair slammed backwards and sideways, rolling her to the hard floor. She looked up and cringed at the expression on the demon's face. Always before, he had been mocking, teasing. This was nothing but pure fury.

Dominic roared and leapt between them. "STOP!"

"Oh shut up, you overgrown handbag." Bjarte narrowed his eyes and smirked. "I think you need a reminder of just who you're dealing with, Abigail."

Her vision went black and then...

She followed Gladys and Melissa out after the service, bracing herself for the ride home. She really didn't want to get in the car with Mrs. Davidson. She needed a few minutes to pull her mask into place. Nothing had changed, after all. Life had been half-truths since the day she made the choice to hide Dominic's existence. She looked down at The Dragon at her heels. "You need to leave," she thought to him.

He looked up with a startled expression. "Why? I've always been here for you, haven't I? Why would you want me gone NOW?"

"I'm a grown-up. That's what you keep telling me." She kept her words in her head as she moved her eyes back to Gladys. "Grown-ups don't have imaginary friends. I have friends, Dominic. I don't need you anymore." The words tore her apart to think. "I don't want to lose anyone else, but I can't hold onto you forever."

"Don't say that!" The fear in his voice cut like a knife. "You can't send me away! We don't know what happens to forgotten imaginary friends!"

"So it's about YOU and not me, then?" She stepped back, keeping away from her great-aunt, Melissa and the Davidsons. This had to be dealt with. "Are you really protecting me, Dommy? Because I'm not sure anymore." Tears burned her eyes. "I trusted you, I always have. Now you need to trust me. You need to go. Please, go!"

"NO!"

The word erupted in her skull along with a world of pain. She grabbed the sides of her head as she hit her knees. Someone screamed and it took her a moment to realize it was her.

The pain echoed in her head. It felt like her skull was going to explode then... nothing. She blinked, surprised to find herself in tears.

Furiously she wiped them away and struggled to clear her vision. When the blur faded she looked up at the smug demon in horror.

"If you don't want me to pull that again," said Bjarte, his voice as cold as the room. "Then I suggest you start showing some respect. Do we..." he paused and leaned down so his nose was inches from hers, "... understand each other?"

She couldn't answer past the shock. She remembered that day, but the events she had just seen, she didn't remember at all. She remembered having a headache after walking out of the service. She remembered Preacher Davidson's assumption that it had been a demon attack.

Bjarte apparently took her silence for agreement. He pulled back to lean against the wall, arms and ankles crossed with a smug smile and said, "I thought so."

"You're a deceiver." Abby forced herself to her feet, righting her chair and leaning on it. By the feel of things, she was going to have a few bruises. She steeled herself. "That's what Aeneas always calls you. A liar. I don't remember that... so why should I believe it? It's just another trick. Another mind game."

His smug grin just grew. "Ask them." He waved a hand toward The Dragon. "Ask your oh-so-wise guardians if you don't believe me."

Dominic's face was twisted in rage. His teeth were still bared and if his tail moved any faster she would worry it might snap off.

Abby looked at The Dragon, at her grandfather's ghost, and whispered, "It's not true. Tell me it's not true."

"He cannot, Abigail." Aeneas appeared beside her, staff in hand. "I cannot. I wish I could."

Bjarte's laughter echoed in the room. "Sorry to bust your bubble, Abs."

Abby was shaking, but not with fear. Anger coursed through her. She clenched her teeth and put her chair back where it belonged, refusing to dignify him with a reply. She opened her laptop back up and went back to trying to look up video game distribution.

The ding of her messenger almost made her jump out of her skin.

RandomWord: What's shaking, Abs?

Me, she thought bitterly. She took a deep breath and tried to compose herself. *I am NOT going to blast Marlon just because SOMEONE had to throw a temper-tantrum!* "Just trying to figure out how to get Path of the Dragon out there," she typed, then resumed looking through the results. Her mind drifted to the conversation in her grandmother's kitchen.

"We're too young!" She fidgeted under her grandmother's gaze and fought to keep her voice low. "We're just..."

"Abby," said Gail, her tone soothing yet firm. "I know it's become fashionable to wait. But I can assure you, the day will come when that boy will ask for your hand. And it will likely be sooner than you think. If you know in your heart you don't want that -"

Irritation washed over her. "I didn't say that!" She tugged at her hair. "Grandma, I've been hearing hints I need to either set a date, or find someone I'm willing to do so with since we started dating. IF he asked..." She closed her eyes. "I'd say yes in a heartbeat." She trusted Marlon. Really, the only one she trusted more was Dominic.

"But if it's any time this year," Gail said as she walked over and cupped her face. "You'll be scrambling to postpone the actual ceremony."

Abby felt her face burn as she nodded rapidly, unable to speak.

"Well," Dominic chimed in with a chuckle. "At least you'd have six-months Pre-Cana in your favor it stall with. Plus if Wasp's lady gets involved, she might take that long just to plan it all."

"He'll wait." Gail smiled knowingly. "He's a Samson; they grasp patience more than most would believe."

"He's also a guy," said Bjarte, breaking through her musing. "You don't satisfy him, he'll get it elsewhere. Wouldn't be surprised if he's already —"

The messenger's ding thankfully interrupted the demon.

RandomWord: Speaking of. Abs? I'm not... Look I'm not trying to take over The Dragon's game. I just want to help.

DragonflyGirl: I know, Mars-Bars. *smiles* I was just surprised the other day. I do appreciate it, really. I just wish I understood how to get it OUT. All these results make no sense.

RandomWord: We'll work something out. By the way, I think I may have solved the mystery of the forum report.

DragonflyGirl: Wait, what? Seriously?

RandomWord: Yeah... check this out. Tell me if you notice anything.

The next message was a link. Abby clicked it and the home page of a site called "The Freakshow" appeared. The introduction on the page was extremely familiar.

The world is not what you have always known. To say it has changed would be a lie; it has always been this way. The only thing that has changed is your eyes are open to it. Humans are not alone in the world. You never really were. Yes, I said "you." I am not human. Most here are not. We may look like you, talk like you, but we are not you. We cannot and never will be.

We hid our differences as best we could. It was not a matter of dishonesty but of survival. Humans have a knack for destroying anything that doesn't fit with their narrow definition of "normal". We are the strange. We are the different. We are the freaks. Maybe you are one too.

Welcome to the Freak Show.

DragonflyGirl: This is... it's a full-blown ripoff of the Sanctuary!

RandomWord: Not really. You weren't around when Sanctuary started, Abs. I was. Check out the founder's name. It's the same person that originally ran the Sanctuary.

She stared at the message. "Are you telling me the FOUNDER reported it?" she typed.

RandomWord: Looks that way. I remember she went to college or something, had to take off for a couple years, so the Queens took over running it "for" her. "Until she got back."

DragonflyGirl: If she came back, why didn't she just take it back over?

RandomWord: Because if an admin goes inactive long enough, a member can "adopt" the site and take over the admin role.

DragonflyGirl: How do we know one of the Queens just didn't use her username?

RandomWord: Well, for starters, they don't erase accounts when they go inactive. Hers is taken. So if I had to guess, she saw the mess the Queens were making and decided to shut them down.

Abby shook her head. "Excuse me if I'm still not amused. If that's what happened, she wiped out all our stuff in the process," she typed. "A little warning would have been nice."

RandomWord: Yeah, I know. But once the Queens "adopted it," there was no way she could take back control. Reporting it to the main site would be the only way to kick them. From what I remember she wasn't as... she was a better admin than the Queens. I'd almost bet we'll all be getting messages inviting us to join.

DragonflyGirl: Joy.

RandomWord: You OK, Abs?

"Aw, look at Prince Charmin', all ready to jump to your aid again!"

"He asked a simple question you –" Abby gritted her teeth. *No taunting the demon. Positive emotions. Think happy thoughts.*

Bjarte snorted. "Want some fairy dust? See if you can really take flight, Dragonfly?"

"Go to Hell," she snapped, typing, "Just tired. Don't worry. Anything goes wrong, you'll be the first to know."

RandomWord: Thanks, beautiful. Cheer up, next month's Halloween! And this time, you can actually join in! *puppy eyes* Can I talk you into dressing up with me? Pleeease?

Abby laughed out loud. "Sure, Mars-Bars," she replied. "But we're gonna have to find something that's not seven shades of cheesy."

RandomWord: Deal. *eyes clock* Not to be a spoilsport but I should crash. I get to help paint the fence tomorrow. Goodnight, Abs. I love you. Sweet dreams.

DragonflyGirl: Good night, Mars-Bars. Love you, too. Behave and I might let you pull a Tom Sawyer on me tomorrow.

RandomWord: Pull a what?

DragonflyGirl: *rolls eyes* I swear, you need to read more than fantasy. The part where he conned the kids with painting the fence?

RandomWord: Oh... that! LOL Now that would be a picture. Check ya later beautiful.

She watched his name go offline with a sigh and a smile. "I need to get to bed anyway." She shut the laptop down. She could look into the game thing later.

CHAPTER 18

Abby put the chairs up one by one and prepared to clean the bar's floor. Sam had turned the volume down on the jukebox before giving her permission to run out the money the customers had put in, so the music set her rhythm. Dominic lay on the stage, watching her as his tail tapped along with the beat.

"First, sweep," she muttered to herself as she matched actions to words. It was amazing the dust and dirt the place could accumulate. "Then mop. Then get out the fans and dry the floor so some idiot doesn't ignore the 'wet floor' sign and sue." She snickered at that last instruction.

"Cinderelly, Cinderelly." Bjarte was back to his keep-out-of-sight-just-to-unsettle-her routine. "Looks like your aunt's training didn't go to waste."

The jukebox stopped. She walked over and scanned the songs. A smirk appeared on her face as she chose the perfect response to the demon's commentary. "Hey, Cinderella," she sang along with a song she remembered hearing at her grandmother's. "What's the story all about? I got a funny feeling we missed a page or two somehow." She laughed at the demon's groan and swept the floor to a continuous stream of country music. When it stopped, she swapped in some Billy Joel.

"Ugh, Abs, seriously?"

She turned to see Marlon shut the front door behind him as he shook his head.

"Please tell me that was something someone already paid for." He locked the door then spun and put his hands in his pockets with a grin. "How ya doin', beautiful?"

"Been better, been worse," she said. Abby leaned on the broom handle and smiled. "You?"

"Same really. It's barely October and everyone's already going crazy with the Halloween crap." He shrugged. "Couldn't really decorate in the complex, so they're going all out this year."

"If that was not 'really' being able to decorate," said Abby as she dumped the dustpan. She turned and headed to the storeroom to swap the broom for the mop. "I'm almost scared to see what 'really' decorating means." She smiled to take the sting out of the words. "So why are you here instead of helping?"

"Well..." Marlon trailed behind her. "My options were keep my brothers from murdering each other or hang with my lady." When she stopped at the door, he kissed her cheek, making her face heat up. He grinned again. "No contest, really." He gently tucked her hair behind her ear. "Need help?"

His touch sent tingles along the skin his fingers brushed... and other tingles went lower than she wanted to admit. She flinched at the wolf-whistle from the demon as he noticed the direction of her thoughts. Abby stuttered, "I... I... You could fill the bucket up if you want."

He stepped back and grabbed it. As he crossed the room, the jukebox changed tracks and Marlon looked at it suspiciously. "Wait... that's the song you're always singin', ain't it?"

I don't think my face can get any hotter. Abby nodded as she grabbed the bleach and the mop. She stayed behind him as he went to the deep sink behind the bar and filled the bucket. She couldn't look at him.

Bjarte just laughed and started singing the chorus, reminding her why she had looked it up in the first place: "Dominic" used to sing it. *So that was him wearing the mask then.*

Marlon sat the bucket down then turned and disappeared into the store room. He came back with a second mop and smiled. "Guy in that song's crazy."

"Huh?" She poured some bleach into the water, stirred it with her hand, then dipped in her mop and started scrubbing.

"You Catholic girls don't start too late, if you ask me." Marlon dipped his mop into the bucket and began to work on the floor. He threw a grin her way. "You move at your own pace."

Abby stared at him.

"Sweet words." Bjarte's voice was amused. "Of course you don't start 'too late,' since he'll be the one cherry-pickin'. Wonder if it's clicked how slow your pace really is?"

Dominic rolled his eyes. "I stand by the succubus suggestion."

"Sometimes, Mars-Bars," she said, putting more force into the mopping than she needed to in an effort to not snap at the demon. "You seem too good to be true."

Marlon didn't reply right away, then he scratched at the back of his head, turned and smiled. "Back at ya, Abs." He then went back to working on the floor.

Abby sighed and shook her head with a fond smile. *Thank God there's only one Marlon.*

"Peace be with you," said the man beside him as he gave a firm handshake.

"And also with you," Marlon said automatically, then sat back down beside his lady. His eyes kept darting over to Abby as he fought to keep from squirming, not that she had ever scolded him for it. He reached up and started toying with the gold cross he wore, then smiled slightly when he realized how he'd picked up the habit. As long as he could remember, whenever Abby was upset, her hand would go to her neck. Whatever pendent she touched first – the locket with her parents' picture or the cross he himself now wore – would be rubbed between her fingers. Now more often than not, her hand found the cross he'd given her.

Abby no longer shared his discomfort, smiling all through the service as she had since her 18th birthday. Davidson's thinly veiled criticism and long-winded tirades were something neither had enjoyed, but at least they'd been united in their opinion of the good preacher.

Now you're on your own, and if you dare tell her you still don't buy this garbage, you can kiss her good-bye. Marlon sighed. It was less not 'buying it' and more just... not understanding. How could anyone believe something and not question it? Abby would most likely hit him, but he had yet to see a real difference between the churchgoers here and Preacher Davidson's flock. All he saw were sheep that would run off the cliff if the shepherd drove them that way.

But not her, he thought, running the cross back and forth across the chain. Abby had never been just a blind follower. Over the years, she had questioned and debated with him, and even admitted things didn't make complete sense. If asked, he said he followed the God Abby did. Because even if she wouldn't admit it, Abby's beliefs were her own brand of religion. *I know there's Something there.* His eyes darted to the ceiling in mute apology. *But uh, Sir? If all these stories are true... no offense, You come off more a tantrum-throwing child than a Father. Still, I'm upholding my end of the deal.* He looked at his lady, happy and well. *You did Yours.*

Since the day he had dared to bargain with "God," Marlon found himself praying whenever his worries got the better of him. Often the last thought he had before he fell asleep was keep her safe. It wasn't the fancy words of the Mass or the prayer books, but it was straight from the heart. Putting up with self-righteous "shepherds" was a small price to pay for that. He was a Samson, and he kept his promises.

"Can you pick up Little Wasp's thoughts?"

"They are none of our business or concern."

Dominic snorted. "That's not what I asked."

"You have asked this several times over," Aeneas replied, eyeing his charge and her suitor. He shook his head at the pageantry surrounding them. "The answer has not changed. He is not our charge, and his path is his own."

"So what I'm getting is his pair can, but not you. This no co-operation policy is one huge flaw in the system, if you ask me." Dominic tapped his tail against the floor. "You wouldn't have needed my help when Screwtape tried his hand at vehicular homicide, if you could have just asked Wasp's for back up."

"I am aware the playing field is far from equal. He has been successful with the tactic before." Aeneas looked sideways at his former charge. "I should have considered he would try it again."

"Is there a pattern?" The Dragon looked at his granddaughter in concern. "He acts like you two go way back. Have you..." He dug his claws into the carpet. "If you've been paired with him as much as he says, haven't you learned what tips the odds in his favor?"

"If I had, I certainly would not voice it, now would I?" Aeneas met Dominic's glare with his own. "I will tell you this much. What damned you, has damned every charge I have ever lost."

"I see." Dominic folded his ears as he thought that over. They both knew what had led to his slip. Love. He had almost accepted the deceiver's offer in his desperation to reach his daughter. Almost, but had recognized Bjarte for what he was and called on the Creator for aid. The loyalty had saved him from the Destroyer, but the selfishness had separated him from his daughter.

Aeneas thought of the boy, ancestor of both "dragonfly" and "dragon," whose form he still wore. Time and again, love had ruined the best laid plans of both guardian and deceiver. His eyes narrowed as his charge's suitor toyed with his cross. *And only time will tell which side love will serve this round.*

CHAPTER 19

"Check ya later, Abs." After Mass, Marlon walked her to the stairs that lead to the deck of her and Sam's apartments. He pressed a quick kiss to her cheek and flashed a grin before getting on his bike and taking off.

Abby shook her head with a fond smile as she watched him go, then started up the stairs. She nearly jumped out of her skin when she heard Sam chuckle.

"Ah, history repeats," he said, leaning against the railing. "Thinkin' how many times I've seen this kinda thing makes me feel old, I swear."

"This kind of thing?"

"You're gonna regret asking that," Dominic told her. He scratched as his chin with a fore-paw, his tail swishing slightly.

"I done seen Wasp pussy-foot around Queenie until he managed to pop the question, and even then he was sweatin' bullets," he replied. "I saw Buzzard tend his sunflower until she bloomed." He rolled his eyes. "At least that's how he puts it. Kid's a chip off the old block and I'm hoping Queenie don't stick me in a new suit when you two finally tie the knot. The old one don't see daylight 'cept for those things so it's like new anyway."

She forced a smile and mumbled a quick good afternoon before she retreated into her apartment. She changed into a pair of sweats and let Domino out of the crate. She got his ball for him and sat on the trunk. "So what are those 'tells' you and everyone else keeps going on about?" Abby asked her grandfather as she kicked the ball between her feet. The excited kitten shook his head and crouched. "Since I am apparently too dense to spot them?"

The Dragon thankfully cut to the chase. "For starters, the bending-over-backwards to cater to you," Dominic replied. He sat beside the trunk, eyes on the kitten. "Both Wasp and Buzzard spoil their ladies as much as they can get away with. And since both are perfectly capable of dealing with most of their problems, their men have to settle for deferring to their choices."

"Like when he says 'whatever you wanna do is fine' instead of voicing an opinion, or 'if you don't want to, we can do something else'," she said, shaking her head. "What else?"

"The over-protective behavior. If I had a dollar for the number of times I had to grab Wasp's arm 'cause some idiot 'insulted' his lady, I could have bought an island." Dominic sighed. "At least yours has more self-control. He hasn't actually punched someone yet."

"No," said Aeneas, amusement obvious in his voice. "But she has."

"Very funny," said Abby.

"The first tell is the one they don't always pick up on themselves: Jealousy."

Abby looked at The Dragon. "Jealousy?"

"Such as when Gladys was trying her best to pair you with the rat and just mentioning it made Little Wasp break something?"

"That was an accident." She had almost forgotten the glass that Marlon had broken on his first visit to her grandmother's. He had dropped the glass right after she mentioned that Gladys was trying to marry her off.

"Samsons tend to be a bit possessive," said Dominic sagely. "You wouldn't quite know it with the arrangement Buzzard's got, but if anyone, say, tried to point out he doesn't need 'extras'..."

"The fur would fly," she finished. "So, protective, possessive, and pampering." She rubbed her head. "Perfect."

"Why you complainin' so much?" Bjarte appeared, folded arms and crossed ankles, leaning against the wall. "Pretty sure a lot of girls would trade ya... and you keep it up, Prince Charming will drop ya for one that appreciates it."

"Would people stop putting words in my mouth? It's sweet... in small doses." She thought of hand-picked flowers, fast-food surprises... She rubbed the cross between her fingers. "How does all that add up to 'he'll be asking for your hand sooner than you think'?" she asked, forcing herself to ignore the demon. "I mean, they were like that with every girl they dated, right?"

"Yes." Dominic shot a glare at Bjarte, then looked up at her. "But they are always playing for keeps. Wasp had a few girls before his lady, but... he was always a mess when it came out they weren't on the same page."

Abby opened her mouth, then stopped herself. She wasn't sure she wanted to know just what he meant by "a mess." The idea of hurting Marlon stung, but if he was expecting wedding bells anytime soon, he was up a creek without a paddle.

"I don't get why ya got a problem with it," said Bjarte with a smirk. "After all, ain't that what all good girls are supposed to be aiming for? Besides, ya said yourself you'd say yes in a heartbeat."

She flinched at the reminder he was *always* around, every bit as much as her guardians. She didn't speak, but the reason came to mind anyway.

And the demon burst out laughing. "Oh, come on! You really think having a few brats is gonna keep ya from your dream job? The way Prince Charming bends over backwards to give ya anything ya want? He'll probably wear the dress himself."

107

"SHUT UP!" Abby's face burned. "I'm not stupid, even though you keep trying to convince me otherwise. When Mom had me she lost her chance at college. I'm not gonna let that happen to me!" She sighed. "Marlon's got career plans of his own, and it wouldn't be fair to ask him to give his up either. Why did this have to come up so soon? I thought we were on the same page!"

"Who says you're not?" demanded The Dragon. "You never talk about anything important."

"Meow!"

Abby looked down to see Domino glaring up at her. Her foot was on his ball and he was trying to snag it with his claws. She had stopped kicking it for him some time during the conversation. His tail tapped the floor much like The Dragon's. She couldn't help laughing. "Bossy little guy, aren't you Dommy?" She nudged the ball away for him and went back to what he clearly viewed as her task. "At least you're easy to please." She looked at her grandfather. "We talk just fine, thank you."

"You beat around the bush, never coming out and saying what's bothering you. Little Wasp's not a mind reader and neither are you."

Her phone, ever on her nightstand charging, rang. She sighed and looked at the caller ID. "No, but apparently his grandmother is." She flipped the phone open. "Hello, Mrs. Samson."

"Good afternoon dear," came Vera's cheery voice. "I hope this isn't a bad time."

"Of course not. How are you?" Abby watched her feet to make sure she didn't accidentally kick her kitten as she kept his ball moving. It took a little more small talk before Vera Samson got to the point.

"I know this is really short notice," said Vera. Her voice, still bright and airy, held the slightest hint that if Abby refused, the older woman would be very disappointed. "But Tura and I were hoping you could join us for lunch?"

Abby shook her head in amusement. "Sure, Mrs. Samson, I'm just hanging out with Dommy right now. Can I meet you somewhere?"

"No, dear, we'll pick you. No need to waste gas, after all. See you in a few."

The call disconnected, leaving Abby staring at the phone. She shut it and looked up at the demon. "Not. One. Word."

Bjarte just grinned and then vanished from sight.

Small talk filled the time as they waited for their orders. Abby fidgeted, toying with her cross once more as she glanced around the dining room. The atmosphere was a lot classier than she was used to and she couldn't help feeling like a duck amid swans.

"You're fine," said Dominic from her feet. "This place ain't the Ritz or nothing, just an old Italian restaurant. Relax."

Easy for you to say, she thought. *I'm the only one that can see you.*

"So how are you and Sam getting along?" asked Vera with a smile. "The old coot driving you up a wall yet?"

"Just fine, Mrs. Samson," she replied. "The jokes get a little old after a while, but then so do mine, so I hear." *Mostly from annoying spiritual advisers.*

Datura looked from her mother-in-law to Abby and back again. "Why do you always have to beat around the bush?" She rested her chin in her hand. "A little birdy told us that you're getting flustered when certain topics come up, so the Queen Bee thought it 'would be wise to discuss these matters and lay to rest the unneeded anxiety.'"

"How many times must I tell you not to call me that?"

"Note she said nothing to refute the statement." Dominic looked up at his best friend's wife with amusement. "The Queen Bee Vera never says anything without reason."

I did, thank you. Abby looked sideways at the two older women. "Meaning?" *And don't one of you,* she thought at her guardians, *tell me I'm being dense this time!*

"I've known you for years." Datura took a quick drink. "And I don't want to hurt your feelings." She smiled. "But you keep quiet for others' sake more than you should. If you don't want to marry my son, please just tell him so. You'll hurt him more if you just let it lie."

"Abigail..." Dominic's tone came out a warning as he picked up her emotional reaction. "Don't do anything I wouldn't do."

Pretty sure I won't. "You know what I find funny?" Abby placed her hands flat on the table, making sure not to slam them down. "The fact Marlon's not said one word about us getting married, yet everyone keeps shoving it in my face and putting words in my mouth."

Datura flinched and suddenly found the table very interesting.

Vera was unfazed. The old woman sipped her drink, then smiled. "Dear, are you aware how Bryan proposed?"

Abby bit her tongue and shook her head.

"He gifted me with what I assumed at the time was a simple token of affection." She pulled a gold chain into view; from it dangled a pendant in the shape of a honey bee at rest upon a flower. "This, Abby dear, was my engagement ring."

"Mine was my namesake pressed into a copy of *The Jungle Book,*" added Datura with a fond smile. "Though Wendel did tuck a 'will you marry me' note in too."

Her hand automatically went, not to the cross, but to the charm Marlon had given her.

"Ah, so you are following." Vera nodded, her smile indulgent and amused. "Yes. History repeats and the tradition continues." She took another sip then looked at her sternly. "You have made it quite clear you are not interested in marriage just yet. If you want to preserve your friendship, I suggest you discuss your concerns sooner rather than later." She sighed. "The poor communication skills come from my side of the family, I hate to admit."

"Gee," said Dominic. "Pretty much what I said about an hour ago."

Did you know what this was? Abby demanded. She stared at the charm, remembering Marlon's reassurance that it was "no big deal." Then her hand went back to the cross. *Then again... maybe* it *wasn't...* She looked up at the two Mrs. Samsons. "I... just one question: does the white knight stuff ever tone down?"

Vera and Datura shared a look and burst out laughing.

CHAPTER 20

Marlon checked the oil, then tightened up the loose parts on his bike. Keeping the thing running in good condition was a pain most days, but worth it. He started it up and let it run for a moment as he double-checked his work, then shut it off.

"If your grandmother caught me workin' on my bike alone, I'd be lucky to get the couch."

Marlon's head jerked around and he found Bryan Samson leaning against the wall beside the door into the house, arms folded and legs crossed at the ankle. The look on his grandfather's face was all too familiar and it took all of his self-control not to take three steps back. He forced a smile that he was sure looked nothing like one. "H-Hey Grandpa. What brings you here?"

"You."

"Me?" Marlon swallowed hard. He wracked his brains to figure out what he'd done lately that would warrant this and came up blank. *Well whatever it was, you brought the old man down on you. So you done f-*

"What ya doin', keepin' secrets from Dragonfly?"

Secrets from Abs? Marlon blinked. "Does not compute, Grandpa."

Bryan sighed, pushed off the wall and came to stand in front of him. "This afternoon V got a phone call from The Dragon's lady. I heard her tellin' Gail she and your mom would set your lady straight since you didn't. What didn't ya tell her that they have to?"

"Acting on stuff ya overhear when someone's on the phone's a real bad idea," he replied, rubbing at the back of his head and cringing at the memory. "Trust me."

"Don't change the subject and answer the question."

"I don't know," he admitted. "I've told Abby almost everything really so..." He couldn't think of anything he'd kept from her. *Better ask Mom. Hopefully Grandma's already called her.* He'd have to work fast to keep them from freaking her out. Sure his mother knew Abby, but his grandmother was intimidating even to him. Whatever it was, it'd be better if he handled it himself instead.

"Well, ya done left something out, or they wouldn't be talkin' to her today."

"TODAY?"

"Did I stutter?"

"What the Hell?!" Marlon looked at his grandfather. "Stupid question, but why are they going to *her* and not *me*? I mean, *I'm* the one that screwed up apparently, right?"

"No idea." Bryan folded his arms and rolled his eyes. "I've never got V's way of dealin' with things. She's gotta have a reason though. She always does."

And her plans always end so well, don't they? Marlon rocked on his heels, every instinct screaming at him to bolt. To rush to his lady's side and shield her. *But she can take care of herself. Hasn't she shown you that?* Yes, but... there was no question being cornered like that would be bad. Very bad.

Bryan looked at his watch. "Considerin' ya'll got school tomorrow, I'm sure they won't keep her too long. Sure you can't think of anythin' you didn't mention?"

"Keep her?" Marlon flinched at the crack in his voice. "Wait, I thought they were just gonna talk!" He rubbed his temples, fighting back the panic those words invoked. "Dang it! I wish I knew what brought this on. I thought things were going pretty good, myself."

"You really think V's gonna talk in an apartment where she can't even sit down?" Bryan rolled his eyes. "She invited Dragonfly to lunch. I did stick around for that. Geez, take a chill pill. It's not like she's – Hey, where are you goin'?"

"Thanks for the heads up, Grandpa," Marlon said, then started up the bike. "But I gotta go." He hit the garage door opener and flew out the driveway, barely remembering to hit the button and close the door behind him. *You realize you don't know where they are? No, but Abs has to come home some time. Hopefully I can straighten this out before...* He couldn't think it. *I swear if Grandma scares her off like she almost did Mom I'll never forgive her.*

"Goodnight, Mrs. Samson, Mrs. Samson." Abby carefully got out of the car and dipped into a curtsy. "I appreciate the advice, though you might want to work on your delivery next time." She smiled. "At least you should have some time, since Kenny's not old enough to date yet."

"Tell that to the girls he sneaks wildflowers to," Datura replied. She rubbed at her temples. "That boy is gonna be heart-breaker I swear."

Vera just smiled. "You take care now, dear. Goodnight."

Abby sighed and looked up at the dirty old building with its halfheartedly-flashing neon sign. What had once frightened her was now a refuge. She walked around to the back, eager to see Domino and curl up under the covers.

"You aren't going to discuss this with Little Wasp?" Dominic's tone radiated disapproval. "How many people have to tell you this before you listen?"

"I'm not talking about something this important on opposite sides of a screen." Abby sighed. He knew her thoughts just like Aeneas and his counterpart did, so there was no use in hiding it. "What if they're wrong? What if you all are? Just because Bryan and Wendel..." She trailed off as she rounded the corner and spotted Marlon's bike parked by the stairs. *Crap!*

"What were you saying about other sides of a screen again?"

She took a step back before remembering there was nowhere to run. She was home and obviously Marlon was waiting on her.

"Hopefully not inside," Aeneas chimed in. "There is a fine line between concerned and controlling, and the boy is dangerously close to the latter."

If his mother and grandmother are to be believed it's inherited. She rocked back on her heels then shivered as an icy breeze brushed past her.

"You're gonna catch a cold standing here like a fool."

"Abs?"

Busted. Abby sighed and looked up to see Marlon leaning on the railing of the porch. "Hey, Mars-Bars." She swallowed hard and started up the stairs. "What brings you here?"

"Grandpa showed up." Marlon looked shamefaced. "He uh, well... he said..." He rubbed his face and shook his head. "What'd I screw up so bad Grandma thought she had to fix it?"

She walked past him and unlocked her door. "Let's get inside before we both get sick." She went straight to the crate and pulled Domino out. She cradled him in her arms and sat on the bed and rocked him, keep her eyes on the kitten rather than her boyfriend.

Marlon didn't let it go. He sat down beside her, not quite touching. "Now I gotta know, Abs. It has to be pretty bad for you to be acting like this." His eyes met hers, a silent plea at odds with the obviously forced smile.

"I swear, Abigail, if you don't just spit it out I'll -"

"Marlon," she said softly, sitting Domino on her lap and reaching up for her cross, "what's this mean?"

He looked confused. "Mean?"

Of course I'm going to have to spell it out. "Why did you give it to me?"

"Because I took yours and you needed a new one." His expression became slightly annoyed. "I told you that when I gave it to you. Plus you're The Dragon's granddaughter."

"OK," she replied, swallowing hard. *Please God, don't let them be wrong.* If they were, if he didn't feel the way everyone thought... She slowly raised her arm and turned it so the charm was in plain view. "How about this? Because your grandmother and your mom seem to think it's an engagement ring." She flinched as Bryan's favorite word came flying out of her boyfriend's mouth. The reaction didn't tell her anything either way though, and she crossed her fingers that it wouldn't be all she got out of him.

"I'm gonna..." Marlon stood up and started pacing, his hands clenched at his sides. "I don't believe this! *Seven Hells!* Why did they have to stick their noses in? I swear!"

"I'll take that as a no," she said softly. She wrapped her arms around her cat, blinking. As much as she had suspected it, it still hurt.

He stopped short and looked at her, the anger falling from his face to be replaced with concern. "Abs... Did they bother to say why they felt the need to say it was?"

"A 'little birdy' told them that I wasn't reacting to the idea of us getting married well." She stroked Domino, fighting to calm her irritation. "Educated guess Grandma or Sam, since both have said something about it."

"Your *grandma* said..." The shock in his voice was obvious. *"WHY?!"*

She'd gone too far to turn back now. Still she chose her words carefully. "According to reputable sources, there's 'tells' when a guy in your family is 'thinking long-term' and you have all of them." She glanced at The Dragon out of the corner of her eye. *Are you happy now? Looks like you were seeing things more often than I do!*

Dominic didn't say a word, one of the few times she'd ever had him remain silent.

"Well, at least they got that part right."

Abby jerked her head up, stunned. "Wait what? They *do?*"

"Uh, yeah..." Marlon scratched at the back of his head, looking nervous but still keeping his eyes on her. "I kinda am..." He shrugged. "I mean, I know it might not work out. And if it don't, I'll live. We'll still be friends after all. Just..." He stared down at his feet. "I'm sorry Abs. But that charm just means you're family. No matter what, you always will be."

She swallowed again, trying to dislodge the sudden lump in her throat. Unable to speak, she patted the spot beside her.

Marlon smiled and obliged, sitting down and keeping his eyes on his hands as he kept them moving. "I get why they'd think that, though. Grandpa and Dad didn't go traditional with theirs. But I..." He shrugged. "Look, it's OK if we're not on the same page."

Those words did it. "Who knows?" she replied, looking at Dominic with a faint smirk. "Maybe we are. We've never talked about it after all."

"That's true." When Marlon looked up, there was hope in his eyes. "So, maybe we should?"

She smiled, then reached out and laid her hand on his. "That sounds like a plan."

"Wanna flip a coin and see who goes first?"

Her laughter shook the bed, startling Domino, who meowed in protest at his suddenly moving position. She stroked him until he started purring. "I don't think that's necessary." Abby looked up into his eyes. *Now or never.* "I love you. You're my best friend, and honestly

I can't see my life without you in it." She took a deep breath. "And like I told Grandma, *if* you asked... I'd say yes in a heartbeat." She held up a finger for him to let her finish. "But I wouldn't want to actually walk down the aisle any time soon. I'm not gonna end up like Mom and miss college."

"I can live with that." His affection for her was written all over his face. He smiled and slowly wrapped his arm around her shoulders. "Best things come to those who wait. Yeah, think we're on the same page now."

Abby leaned in and rested her head on his shoulder. "Thank God."

"Yeah," said Marlon as he wrapped her in a hug and tucked her head under his chin. "Really."

CHAPTER 21

"It never stops, they just get better at hiding it." Abby repeated Vera and Datura's advice to herself as she sat in front of her laptop after school. She flipped between search results for couple's costumes and for game distribution, growing more frustrated by the second. "So you distract them with something else. Give them a task to do. Something that makes them feel helpful but keeps them out of your hair." She tilted her head at a couple costumes from an anime and thought of the cards she still kept in her trunk. "We could go as Jessie and James..." She laughed. "Oh! Jessie, James... Now I get it!"

"It took you this long, what with Cowboy's real name?" Dominic rolled his eyes.

"Spoilsport." Abby's gaze stopped on an ad for an "indie game" contest. She clicked the link and scanned the rules. "This looks promising." The prizes included a distribution contract. She smiled as the messenger dinged. "Perfect timing."

RandomWord: Hey, beautiful. What are you up to?

DragonflyGirl: Costume searching and game researching. Look what I found.

She linked the contest, crossing her fingers it was a good idea. If anyone would know, it was Marlon. He ate, slept, and breathed video games. When he didn't reply right away, she started fidgeting. Hopefully that was a good sign.

RandomWord: Whoa.

DragonflyGirl: Good or bad?

RandomWord: It's a long shot, but if The Dragon's game could win this, you'd def have an audience waiting. Still... the game itself isn't all you need, you know that right? This is asking for a game book, cover art...

Abby smiled as an idea occurred to her. "Stuff you're good at?" she typed, hoping he'd take the bait.

RandomWord: Damn straight! Er, I mean, well, uh yeah. *checks the deadline* Yeah, I could do this... If you want me to, that is. I mean...

"You're terrible," said Dominic, shaking his head.

"It's a compromise," she said simply. "We both win." Then she typed, "I don't have a clue how to do half this stuff. If you can pull it off, it would be much appreciated."

RandomWord: I can't promise it'll win, Abs, but I'll give it my best shot.

DragonflyGirl: Sounds like a plan to me. *smiles* So what are you up to, Mars-Bars?

RandomWord: Nothing much, just got done with my homework.

DragonflyGirl: That's good. Well, I hope the store has better choices than what I'm finding online so far. Some of this stuff for women looks more like lingerie.

When Marlon didn't answer right away, she reread what she said realized it could be misunderstood. *Oh, great, we just got through one misunderstanding.* After ten minutes, she typed, "Mars-Bars?" She sat there for another ten before he finally replied.

RandomWord: Sorry, had to keep my brothers from putting a hole through the wall. Hate to break it to you, Abs, but unless you're ten or something, girl costumes tend to be on the... Don't shoot the messenger, but modesty is the last concern the designers have.

DragonflyGirl: Come on, it can't be that bad!

RandomWord: Don't say I didn't warn you.

Abby stared at the choices in front of her, trying to hide her exasperation with whoever designed the dang things. "This is ridiculous!"

Marlon was clearly trying not to laugh. "Oh, come on! You could pull off some of these."

She spun, facing him. "Marlon Samson!" She put her hands on hips. "The only people who'd want to wear this..." Words failed her. "Anyway, they'd have to work in a strip club!"

"You work in a bar," he replied with a smirk. "It's not too far off."

"What happened to not wanting to go to jail?" She folded her arms across her chest. "You didn't want me out in public in –"

"Who said anything about in public?" The look he gave her made her face heat up.

"MARS-BARS!"

"Told ya the boy wants between your legs."

You stay out of this Screwtape! Abby struggled not to scream the words at the demon. She opened her mouth to scold her snickering boyfriend, but he beat her to it.

"Abs, chill. I was teasing. Sheesh." Marlon's expression went soft. "Look, we can bail on this. Grandma or Dad'll make you whatever you want."

"I know," she replied, grateful her frustration could be written off for the situation itself. "But I don't even know what to dress up as. I swear, this is..." Abby threw up her hands. She started flipping through the racks again. "This shouldn't be this complicated!"

Dominic walked over and sat beside her. "He pretty much told you it would be like this." He sighed. "I think your mom read you that Ernie book too many times. Just because you can do everything yourself doesn't mean you have to."

"Hey, how about this?" Marlon smirked as he pulled a nun costume out. Then he ducked as she tried to slap him. "Kidding, kidding!" He looked around and pulled down cat ears and a tail. "Maybe go as Ava?"

"And you as Brock?" Abby smiled when he nodded. "I think our RP characters qualify as cheesy."

Dominic rolled his eyes.

"Maybe, but it's cheesy not sleazy." Marlon grinned then leaned over and quickly kissed her cheek. "Look, just... what did you always want to be but knew you never could?"

"I never really thought about it," Abby admitted, grateful her face was still flushed from the commentary earlier so it wasn't as obvious this time. "No point in daydreaming about something I'd never get to do anyway."

Marlon looked at her sideways then shook his head. "Right, the closest Mrs. Lynde gets to celebrating is helping Davidson with his Christian version of a haunted house."

"Hell House," Abby corrected automatically. She shivered at the memory of the one time Gladys had taken her. The tall flames leaping from the braziers as "evil" laughter and screams pumped in from speakers filled the room flashed through her mind. It was the stuff of nightmares and she had screamed and caused such a fuss that Gladys had arranged for her to see her grandmother on Halloween from then on.

"You were robbed of a proper childhood," said Dominic with a slight growl. "Shared candy and TV specials instead of actual experience."

It wasn't that bad, she told him. *At least I got to spend more time with Grandma.*

"Abs?" Marlon reached out and waved his hand in front of her face. "Earth to Abby." His expression became concerned. "You OK? Look, if ya ain't comfortable with this —"

"Mars-Bars." She fought not to groan. "I didn't say that." She flipped past a Cinderella costume, then a knock-off of a familiar yellow gown. *If only relationships were as easy as the fairy tales.* She was honestly tempted, though. Then at least the demon would have a good reason to refer to her boyfriend as "Prince Charming". "Look, let's split up. Call me if you find anything that makes sense, OK?"

They stayed until the store closed and went home empty-handed.

CHAPTER 22

By the next Sunday, Abby was regretting following the advice of her "future in-laws." With Marlon so engrossed in preparing for the game contest, the most she saw of him was in class. He hadn't picked her up since last Tuesday and he wasn't even at the door to meet her anymore. Their chats now consisted of "what do you think?", "is this OK?" and "working", if that. He still replied at least, but she missed actual conversation.

"You wanted him to tone it down," Dominic reminded her. "Don't complain now."

"Tone it down, yes," she said, rubbing the cross between thumb and forefinger as she paced. "Stop completely, no. I haven't seen him this obsessed since the last TCG Tournament. At least then I could help him practice." She looked at the clock. "He should have been here by now."

"Why attend a boring service when he's a got 'his lady's' task to perform?" Bjarte appeared, sitting on her trunk with a grin. "You just gave him an easy-out, since he knows how much stock you put in that pile of trash."

"Guess the fact the game is a testament to the fact you lost gets to you." Abby glanced at the phone on her nightstand. If Marlon didn't show up soon she would break down and call him.

The demon burst out laughing.

Abby folded her arms and narrowed her eyes. "Mind letting me in on the joke?"

"Just that I still can't believe Annie got him to rewrite history so well." Bjarte's smile would have fit the snake as it looked at Eve. "Didn't ya figure out why the 'hero' is a dead ringer for that stick in the mud?"

"Because the two of you couldn't resist screwing with my

dreams," replied Dominic with a growl. "Seeing you two battle it out night after night, figured I might as well put the images to use." He smirked. "And blonds are stereotypical heroes, so flipping that helped my message."

"You want to tell 'em, Annie?" The demon looked behind her at the guardian, smug as ever. "Or should I?"

"Aeneas, what is he going on about?" Abby walked past the bed and grabbed the phone. *If I wait much longer, I'll miss Mass myself.* She listened to the phone ring, trying not to count each one. She had never known Marlon to just skip something without warning.

"The game's story line bears a marked resemblance to that of my first charge," came the reply. "He had a brother who made a bargain for power whom he tried to save."

"And he failed not only the brother but himself," added Bjarte. "Him defeatin' me is a bunch of crap. So much for the truth."

"You would do well to remember that without the correct answer, the player is forced to kill his brother or die himself."

She ignored them. *Pick up, Mars-Bars!* She rubbed the cross and started to pace. *What was wrong that he...*

"Hullo?"

She sighed. "Kenny," she said. "Why are you answering Marlon's phone? Where is he?"

"Cause the ringing is annoying. Marlon's zonked out."

Her worry turned to irritation. "He's asleep?"

"Uh-huh. Didn't go to bed until the sun was up."

Abby bit her tongue. *It's not his fault his brother pulled an all-nighter.* "Thanks Kenny, I gotta go. You be good now, OK?" Once the phone disconnected she snapped it shut and put it back on the nightstand. "Awake until dawn, knowing Mass is in the morning." She felt like swearing but couldn't spare the money for the jar. She grabbed her coat and headed for the door. Let him sleep in. She wasn't missing it.

"Maybe you should have sat this one out," said Dominic. He sat at her feet as she unlocked the car after Mass ended. "I don't think your mind was here anyway."

I am not going to miss Mass just because Marlon couldn't... Abby jerked the door open. *I've told him a thousand times he didn't have to come. Maybe now he'll stop forcing himself.*

"More likely he will berate himself for failing to keep his word."

Abby gritted her teeth. *His sense of honor is admirable but it's...* She threw her purse to the floor in front of the passenger seat. *He makes himself do stuff just because it's "right" and it's not fair to him!*

The Dragon looked at her sideways as he climbed into the car and sat down. "Do you ever stop and consider what you say?"

Before she could answer, another voice joined the conversation. "Excuse me, child?" The priest came up beside her. "I couldn't help but notice you're without your usual company today. I hope nothing's wrong..."

"No, Father, all's well." Abby bit her cheek to control her temper. "Marlon just couldn't make it this week, I'm sorry." She accepted his well-wishes and agreed to pass them along. Then she got in the car. "If that had been Davidson, he'd have given me a long lecture about how we are all sheepdogs and have to make sure our fellow sheep don't forget their duties."

"He'll come close if Little Wasp goes AWOL permanently." Dominic laid his head on his paws. "Catholic doesn't automatically equal sane, you know."

She forced herself to focus on the road. "I kinda hope he does. Marlon doesn't like being here no matter what he says." She came up on a fast food place and an idea occurred to her. With a smile, she pulled into the drive through. *Turnabout's fair play.* How many times had Marlon brought her meals? She really didn't know as it was one of his favorite things to do for her, and one of the more endearing. It was high-time she returned the favor.

"And this has nothing to do with making sure he's all right?"

Abby made a point to bump the dragon with her purse as she pulled it from the floorboard. "I didn't say that now, did I?" She got her order, then crossed herself as she headed to her boyfriend's house. "Even if it does, it's none of your business."

CHAPTER 23

"Ah-bee!" Isaac came running up to her and hugged her skirt. "Marlon still not up yet. And I wanna play but Momma says can't play and..."

Abby laughed and patted the little boy's head. "Well, I'm here to see him, so he better get up." She knelt down and whispered, "Can you show me how to get to your room? I still get lost here."

Isaac grinned and nodded, taking her hand and dragging her down the hall. He went straight to the room he shared with his brothers, pushed the door open and hit the light switch. Before Abby could stop him, he ran and jumped onto the bed beside his eldest brother. "Marlon!" he shouted, bouncing the mattress, "Ah-bee here!"

"Isaac!" Marlon jerked upright, muttering under his breath. "Kid, stop, you know you're not allowed to jump on the..." He looked toward the door, saw her standing there, and slapped his forehead. "Crap! What time is it? I..."

"Take a chill pill, Mars-Bars," she said, smiling. "You already missed Mass. It's almost noon."

"Seven Hells!" He shook his head, then pushed his brother off the bed. "OK, squirt, you done your good deed for the day. Amscray!"

"But I wanna play!"

"We can play later, Isaac," said Abby gently. She moved back from the door and gestured down the hall. "I think your brother needs some time to wake up anyway." Once Isaac was out of sight, she held up the paper bag. "Hungry?"

"Dang it, Abs, I'm sorry." Marlon shook his head. "I don't even remember when I crashed..."

"Dawn, according to your brother this morning." She stepped into the room and sat beside him on the bed. She pulled a sandwich out of the sack and held it out to him. "No offense, but are you sure you aren't undiagnosed OCD?"

Marlon unwrapped the sandwich, took a bite, and then swallowed. "What?" He looked at her sideways.

"Every time you have a project, you get so focused on it, you forget everything else." Abby took out her own sandwich, but just stared at it. "The world could fall down around you and you'd never notice."

"Abs, that contest ends next Friday."

She looked up at him, thrown for a loop.

"Didn't look too close did ya?" Marlon took another bite. He took his time chewing, swallowed and said, "I know you trust me on things, but there's a reason I'm busting my butt to get this done. Most of the stuff they want I had, but the few I don't takes time."

"Which you don't have, since you work after school." Abby wanted to smack herself. Marlon's job wasn't a three-days-a-week deal like her own. "Dang it, maybe I'm the one with my head..."

"At least working at that game store gives him a better understanding of what sells," Dominic said, curling up at her feet.

"I didn't say that, don't put words in my mouth." Marlon started ripping up his sandwich, his eyes narrowing. "I get I screwed up. I don't need you to come rub my nose in it."

"You didn't –"

"Like Hell I didn't!" Marlon's expression made her scoot backwards. "I made a f-" His grandfather's favorite word flew out of his mouth and she flinched. "-ing promise and didn't keep it, did I?"

"You owe Felice a dollar," Abby said softly, reeling. "Mars-Bars —
"

"Don't 'Mars-Bars' me!" He stood up, dumping his breakfast on the floor. "I know damn well I can't be the goody-two-shoes Catholic." He glared down at the mess he'd made and kicked the food out from under his feet. "I might as well kiss this whole thing good-bye! Don't worry about it, I'll be there next week, and I'll get this crap done. Somehow."

Abby felt her mouth fall open. *Did he really just... where did...* "Where the HELL did you get that idea?" She jumped to her feet, her sandwich joining his on the floor. "Marlon Samson, you listen to me and you listen good! I've known you for how many years? I've told you *how* many times you don't have to come? Dammit, I know you'll never be a Christian, never mind a Catholic, you idiot, and I don't want you to be. You wouldn't be YOU!"

His eyes bugged out and his mouth fell open.

"I love YOU, you idiot! If I wanted some stick-in-the-mud Christian, I'd be with one! For the love of MEW, Marlon!"

Marlon burst out laughing. "Mew? Seriously Abs? *MEW?*" He braced his hands on his knees, doubling over as he laughed like a madman.

Abby watched him for a moment before folding her arms. "I think you need more sleep. I'd say some food in your system, but I wouldn't trust it off the floor of a room shared by three boys, especially when one of which is under three years."

"You're really OK...," Marlon said once he'd sobered, "bein' yoked with a non-believer'?"

"No," she replied, rolling her eyes. "I'm OK being yoked with you. Don't make me 'Gibbs' slap' some sense into you."

"Still..." He hung his head, nudging the food into a pile with his foot. "I made a promise and —"

"I hear one more word about this damn promise and I'm gonna knock you into next week and you can catch Mass early." Abby glared at him. "What the Hell did you say in that promise anyway?"

Marlon mumbled under his breath, eyes on the floor.

"So I can hear you, please."

"Keep her safe. If she's OK... I'll go to church with her. Just please let her be OK."

Abby ignored the heat that came to her cheeks. That he was so desperate to protect her he had said that to Something he doubted existed... "I don't hear 'forever.' You went to church with me for two years plus." She smiled. "I think you're even."

"What if it's all that makes sure you're OK when I'm not there?"

"For a kid of little faith, Prince Charmin' sure puts a lot of stock in bargains." Bjarte's voice made her flinch. "Might want to let him keep it. So he don't give himself a heart attack."

Since when do you encourage... Abby clenched her fists, realizing. *If he has to come to Mass... he won't have time to finish the entry. You don't want to risk the game coming out.*

"Dream on, Dragonfly. You put more stock in that game than P.C. does his promises."

"Marlon..." Abby closed the distance and wrapped her arms around him. "You don't make deals with God. He supposedly listens to what's in here." She pulled back and rested a hand on his heart. "You don't need to do more than ask, if that's what makes you feel right."

His arms wrapped around her and he rested his chin on her head. "I liked it better when you were next door, Abs. Then if stuff hit the fan, someone could be there in a heartbeat. Even if it wasn't me. Now..."

"Now I'm living next to your grandfather's 'father,' and I have a phone that can call for help if I need it." She smiled. "Do you honestly think Sam would let anything happen? He said himself if anything happens to me, the wasps would have his head." She laughed.

"And there won't be enough left for the Buzzard," said Wendel from the doorway. "You two done with the spat? Cause I think a few people at Broad and High didn't hear ya." He eyed the floor with a frown. "Son, you dang well better clean that up before Isaac finds it."

"DAD!"

"If ya wanted privacy, shoulda shut the door. Now, Tura's fixed lunch and seeing as your breakfast is ruined, I suggest you both join us."

Abby laughed and shook her head. "Yes, Mr. Samson." She knelt and gathered up the sandwiches into one of the wrappers and tucked it into her pocket. Domino would enjoy it at least. "Come on, Mars-Bars."

Marlon followed after her, muttering something that sounded like "Hell of a wakeup call."

CHAPTER 24

The welcome interruption of the messenger's ding made Abby smile as she looked up from her math homework. Then she sighed as she saw it wasn't Marlon. *These days just drag on, I swear.*

PlumFelidae: So when am I going to get pictures of your fur baby?

DragonflyGirl: Sorry, I forget to mail them out, this month's been pretty hectic.

PlumFelidae: You know, if I hadn't known better I'd assume you and Random eloped or something. He's been MIA at the Freakshow for... I've lost track.

Abby groaned. "Isn't it bad enough Grandma and the Samsons are stuck on wedding bells? Do I really need to hear it from my online friends too?"

"Pretty sure Miss Kitty was teasing," said Dominic.

PlumFelidae: So when are you coming back to the game? It's not the same without you. :) We felines are rather underrepresented. LOL

DragonflyGirl: I'm not sure I want to come back. What's stopping her from pulling the plug again? That was a lot of work down the drain.

PlumFelidae: ^^; Yeah... I get that, but... really you wouldn't believe how well the game runs now. Hasn't Random told you?

DragonflyGirl: He's been busy. So how have you been?

After a few minutes of small talk, Plum said good-bye for the day, mentioning she had homework to do... provided she could get her own cat off her books. Abby shook her head, ready to finish off her own homework when the messenger dinged again

WaterHorse: Long time no see Ava. :)

DragonflyGirl: Why do I have a feeling me returning to the game has been a topic of conversation lately?

WaterHorse: *shifty eyes* Nooo...

The messenger dinged yet again Abby put her head in her hands. "What is this, Grand Central Station?"

RaspberryRaposa: Hey Dragonfly! So when can we expect to see the puddy tat come back? Ain't seen the terrier for a while either.

DragonflyGirl: *rolls eyes* I'm sorry, it's just seeing years' worth of work wiped like it was trash is unsettling. Random's been busy, I don't see him much either.

She copied and pasted the reply to WaterHorse. "I do miss the game," she said aloud. "But... you know, you put all that work into something only to have it ripped out from under you..."

"You sure you're talkin' about the game?" Bjarte's voice made her skin crawl. "Sounds a bit like you're talkin' about all the effort you and Prince Charming's put in."

"The 'effort we've put in' can't just be erased with a few words." Abby reminded herself that there was no point in getting angry with the demon. "Take a hike, Screwtape."

WaterHorse: I agree it could have been handled better, but there won't be a repeat. The admins actually have more than half a brain between them now.

RaspberryRaposa: It's not gonna happen again, the Queens are dead, long live the Queen! :) I mean, yeah everything being wiped sucked, but it's worth it to have admins with common sense.

"If I didn't know better I'd say these two were the same person sometimes." Abby shook her head and replied to both, "I can agree with that. I'll think about it, OK? Right now I've got a lot on my plate and so does Random."

RaspberryRaposa: You two aren't making wedding plans are you? It was seriously weird when Jenner told us he'd gotten hitched. I mean, barely out of high school? Yeesh!

Abby fought the urge to smack her head against the desk. She typed, "Not yet we're not. Please don't go there, his family and mine are already drowning me in that."

RaspberryRaposa: Whoa, geez, family's crazy huh? I wish we could at least do a group chat... RP that way...

DragonflyGirl: I'd be lucky if my laptop didn't blue screen.

WaterHorse: So where's Random? Ain't seen him for a while.

"Maybe Marlon's right and I do need to get a new laptop," she said as she tapped her fingers against the desk. "All this repeating myself is getting old." She typed, "Random's been busy, he'll be back eventually. I'll think about coming back, but I've got a lot going on right now." Her friends logged off, leaving her alone again.

"Marlon are you ready yet? It can't be that bad." *Or maybe it is. I wonder who got the bright idea for us to dress as the Prince and Princess of Candy Land.* Abby stared into her mirror. Her own costume seemed to steal its pattern from the dress the mice had made Cinderella, but the fabric was covered in fun-sized chocolate bars.

"I'm decent, but I look like the jester, not the prince." She heard him step out of her bathroom. "I say we go looking for next year's ASAP. I can't deal with Dad pulling this twice."

"Your dad said it wasn't his idea."

"Yeah, well, it sure ain't Grandma's. I'm surprised she let this happen."

"That's neither here nor –" Abby turned to look at him and felt her mouth go dry. Yes, his costume was made with the same fabric hers was, but it fit him so well that it accentuated every curve of his frame, especially… She put the brakes on that train of thought before her face could get any hotter. "There."

"Well, will you look who actually has hormones." Bjarte's laughter was like a cold shower. "You know, I gotta agree. Boy looks good enough to eat."

No one asked for your opinion, Screwtape!

"Whoa, Abs," said Marlon, looking her up and down. "Well, I might look like a fool but you sure don't." He let out a slow whistle then walked over, bowed over her hand, and kissed it before standing back up with a laugh. "Might not look like the Prince but I can do the act."

Abby laughed and took his hand in hers. "We better get downstairs before your parents come up after us." She headed out the door with him right behind her. They made it as far as the stairs before she stumbled over the hem of her dress. Marlon caught her before she could fall, pulling her back against him. "Thanks, I…" Her face burned as she realized she wasn't the only one that needed a cold shower. She looked back over her shoulder, certain that her expression betrayed her sudden panic if her heartbeat didn't.

"No prob-" Marlon's grin slid from his face when he saw the look on hers. His eyes darted downwards, he blushed and he stepped back instantly. "Problem." He shifted, scratching at his neck and avoiding her gaze. "Uh, ladies first?" He gestured down the stairs.

Abby pulled up her skirt, making sure she wouldn't trip again and nodded. *Why am I… it's not like… I mean…* She tried to make sense of her scrambled thoughts.

"Why are you so disturbed by what you obviously knew?" Aeneas asked, saying what her frazzled mind refused to. "Perhaps because your great-aunt convinced you that even considering physical intimacy was —"

OK, this officially passed 'awkward' into 'stranger than fiction,' she thought, cutting Aeneas off and fighting to keep from blushing again. *My guardian angel is discussing sexual attraction. That's something I wouldn't have seen coming.*

"At the rate you're going," Bjarte chimed in, "it's not the only thing you won't see coming."

"Your puns are almost as bad as your understanding of human nature," Dominic snapped. "I say both of you shut up and let them handle this. They're doing pretty good on that, now that they're actually talking about the problems for a change."

Abby ignored all three of them, opening the door to the bar before Marlon could reach it and heading inside, hoping the party would be the distraction they both clearly needed.

CHAPTER 25

"Are you gonna avoid me all night?"

Abby looked up from her seat at the bar to find Marlon at her shoulder. He was standing a bit closer than normal. She took a quick drink to give herself time to find words that wouldn't be completely rude. When she couldn't think of anything, she replied, "No."

Marlon swirled the drink in his glass, sat it down, and took the seat beside her. "Could have fooled me." He folded his arms on the bar and looked at her sideways. "You've barely looked at me since we came in. Abs, what's eating –?"

"What's eating me?" Abby forced herself not to slam the glass down. "I don't know, maybe the fact that every single member of your family won't stop making in-law jokes?"

He flinched. "They're just teasing. It's no big deal."

"Maybe to you," she replied, closing both hands around her glass and staring into her drink like it was a crystal ball. "But Grandma would be doing the same thing if she were here and you know she wouldn't be 'just teasing.'"

"It doesn't matter what they say." Marlon mirrored her, taking his own drink in both hands as well. "We're on the same page right? We know where we stand. So..." He tapped his fingers against the glass, eyes locked on the slight movement of the liquid. "Is that the only reason?"

"Go on," came Bjarte's mocking voice. "Tell Prince Charming all about how ya ain't ready to risk a few brats in case it ruins your precious career goals. And watch him say he'll stay home like a good little, whipped boytoy."

Marlon is not a – Abby forced her hands off the glass for fear she'd shatter it. *No one asked for your opinion, Screwtape!*

"That don't stop me from having one."

"Never mind," said Marlon, shaking his head. "Just... Abs, you can tell me anything, you know that right?"

"I know I can trust you, Mars-Bars." Abby sighed. *It's me I don't trust,* she thought, unsure if she should voice that. She knew what he'd say, most likely. He'd tell her she had nothing to worry about, that it was all going to be fine... *But he doesn't know.* She ran a finger around the lip of her glass. *He'll never know what I'm dealing with.* She couldn't tell him about the guardian, the deceiver, or the dragon. He'd never believe it, and she'd already been thought insane once.

"You're gifted, not crazy." Dominic lay curled up by her stool, head on his paws. "Childhood innocence kept into adulthood, nothing more."

"I dunno," chimed in Bjarte. "She sure talks to things no one else can see a lot."

"Good," Marlon said, smiling. "So does that mean I can ask you to dance?" He ducked his head and looked up at her through his lashes. "Pleeeassse?"

She couldn't help it and laughed. "You and those puppy eyes, I swear." She downed the rest of her drink, then followed him to the dance floor. "This sounds weird, but I missed you."

Marlon's hands rested on her shoulder and the small of her back as she tucked her head under his chin. "Yeah," he said, "I missed you, too. But the contest's handled now, so..."

Abby relaxed against him, letting him guide her across the floor. She had always felt safe with Marlon, and with the contest entry finally in, she was looking forward to sharing his company again. Then she realized their closeness wasn't necessarily relaxing for *him*.

"I dunno." Bjarte's voice broke through her brain freeze. "Looks like Prince Charmin' is pretty happy with the arrangement to me."

Marlon flinched when Abby did, his easy smile turning to panic. "Shhh. It's OK, Abs. I'm..." He gave her a sheepish smile. "I'm kinda used to it. Relax, I ain't gonna try anything."

"Used to it?" she hissed, fighting to keep her voice down. "Marlon Samson!"

"Must you emulate the crow calling the raven black?" Aeneas chimed in, his tone scolding. "He interests you in much the same way, yet would you take it any further than idle thoughts?"

That's not the point! Abby started to pull away, hoping not to draw attention their way and embarrass herself further.

"Abs, please!" The fear in his voice made her stop short. "That... look, I... come on." He looped his arm through hers and guided her to a shadowy corner out of sight of the crowd. "That came out wrong. Please, hear me out, OK?"

Abby flinched at the pain in his eyes, but still turned around and bolted out the front door. She couldn't face him or the crowd right then. She leaned up against the wall by the door, taking deep breaths as she fought to calm down.

"Dang, all hot and bothered ain't ya?" The demon's laughter had her digging her nails into her palms. "So is it just P.C. that gets to ya or are you into blonds?"

"Even if she was," said Dominic in a bored tone as he looked at his claws. "You wouldn't even make the long list, deceiver."

I can speak for myself, thank you. Abby clenched her fists and closed her eyes. *Go away, Screwtape, I've more important things to think about than your temper-tantrums.*

"Abs?"

Marlon's voice made her jump and her eyes flew open only for her heart to lodge in her throat. She had never seen him look so... Abused dogs in commercials came to mind.

"I... I'm sorry. I just..." He walked over and leaned against the wall beside her, hands deep in his jacket pockets. "It's... it's just not a big deal to me."

"Marlon," she said softly. "I feel like a hypocrite right now, it's not like..." She swallowed hard and forced the words out. "Like you don't affect me the same way. It's just..."

Sirens rang out and they both looked up to see an ambulance and a fire truck race down the street.

Marlon's gaze followed them until they were out of sight, eyes narrowing. "That was the way to Davidson's church... wasn't it?"

Abby froze. The pungent stench of smoke tickled her nose. "Aunt Gladys never misses the..." Davidson's fiery displays proved he took "Hell House" well beyond the standard nightmare fuel and scare tactic propaganda of his fellow preachers. With the streetlights, it was impossible to be sure, but Abby thought she could see a column of smoke against the dark sky. She slid down the wall and put her head in her hands. Sharp pain struck between her shoulder blades and the pressure on her chest made it hard to breathe. She fought to keep the images of the church ablaze at bay. *Please let me be wrong.* Abby felt a chill that had nothing to do with the October air. Her great-aunt had never missed the Hell House. If she was at the church... and it had caught fire... *If nothing else, let everyone be safe. Please!*

"Wouldn't that be something?" Bjarte's voice made her jerk. "Now all we need is for your gram's place to go up and all your family will —"

SHUT UP! Abby folded her arms as she shook. She startled herself with the venom she felt. She flinched when Marlon sat down beside her, then leaned in when he slowly wrapped his arms around her, silently offering what support he could. The faint smell of the candles burning in the Jack O' Lanterns tickled her nose and made her want to throw up. It called to mind a smoke-scented yard and charred treasures thrown away.

"Why do you care anyway? You ain't spoken to the old bat in months."

She didn't answer him. She couldn't. No good could come of agreeing with the demon... and yet she did. *She's still Grandma's sister.* Abby tucked her head under Marlon's chin and forced herself to focus on the safety she felt with him and nothing else.

CHAPTER 26

I'm glad I still had Melissa's number. Melissa had confirmed Abby's worst fears seconds before assuring her Gladys hadn't been inside. Abby had bought a newspaper the next day, and the picture in the paper showed the scene all too well. She had almost called Gladys three times in the week following the fire, but had chickened out at each attempt. *She doesn't want to hear from me anyway.*

Now Abby sat at her desk, stroking Domino, as she reread the accompanying news story that gave a one-sided version of the life of Preacher Davidson. It also stated the date of his funeral – that day – and that church services would now be held at a neighboring church until the building could be restored. These services would be led by the good preacher's son, who, despite his grief, was taking over his father's role while finishing his higher education.

"The news outlets seem to have a different definition of 'facts' than they did in my day," said Dominic as he looked over the story.

"It doesn't matter," she replied. "No matter what he was, he was Drew's father, and he didn't deserve to die like that."

"Way he lived," Bjarte chimed in, "was probably just a preview of coming attractions."

"No one asked you." Abby turned the paper over, unable to look at the blackened building any longer. Her mind kept replacing the page with the one in Wendel's scrapbook. *I wish Marlon would get here.* For Drew's sake, she didn't want to consider that the demon might be right. The preacher hadn't been a saint by any means, but still.

"You're going to have cat hair all over your dress," scolded Dominic. "You ought to put him in the crate and get the lint roller."

"The dress is black, a few black hairs aren't going to be that obvious." A loud knock at her door made her jump, which startled Domino. "Be careful what you wish for," she muttered under her breath as she watched him vanish under the bed. She picked up her purse, walked over and let Marlon inside.

Marlon was dressed in a black sweater with matching slacks and dress shoes. He looked uncomfortable, but he was there and it meant more to her than he likely knew. "Ready to go?"

"Almost. Domino just bolted on me. Hold on, I'll get him." She walked over to the bed, then looked at the purse in her hand. *Dang it, what was I thinking?* She knelt beside the bed, dropping her purse beside her. "Come on, boy." She could see his eyes shining in the dark, but no matter how hard she tried, she couldn't reach him. "Dang it, Dommy! Get over here!"

"I don't think that will help too much," said The Dragon as he sat beside her.

I didn't mean you, smart Alec!

Marlon came and knelt beside her. "You go and try to get that cat hair off, Abs," he said as he crouched and reached under the bed. "And I'll see if I can get him. If all else fails he'll be safe enough until we get back."

"It's black. No one's going to notice," she replied, then looked at the clock. "I guess he'll be OK but we won't if we don't get going." She picked up the umbrella by the door. *Dang it, my purse!* She turned around to find Marlon beside her, purse slung over his shoulder.

"What do you have in this thing? Bricks?" He slipped a hand under the strap and made a face. "Geez, you'll be lucky if you don't mess up your shoulders carrying this."

"I'll empty it out after I get home, come on." She sighed, thinking of her great-aunt's reaction to her presence. "Let's get this over with."

"The Lord is my shepherd, I shall not want."

"Drew's nailed this so far," whispered Marlon. "If I didn't know better I wouldn't even know they were related."

"Tell me about it." Abby clutched her purse tight as they watched the coffin lowered down into the earth. The only funeral that she could remember attending was her parents', and she had not been allowed to the graveside. The irony of Preacher Davidson sharing the same fate was not lost on her. *Or Preacher Davidson Senior, I should say.*

The service went off without a hitch, and strangely without spiritual commentary. Just as everyone was leaving, she heard Gladys call out, "Abigail?"

"Should have known you couldn't get out of here without running into the old bat."

Dommy, please. Abby sighed. "Marlon, would you please go get the car?" She looked over and waved to her great-aunt. "I'd rather we –"

"Not give them more to talk about," he finished, nodding. "Sure, Abs." His hands went into his pockets as he turned and walked away.

"Still with that Samson boy, I see," said Gladys, clicking her tongue as she stopped in front of Abby. "I must say I can't believe you had the nerve to show up here. Have you no shame at all?"

"I'm here for Drew, Aunt Gladys." Abby ignored the low growl of the dragon beside her. "He's still a good friend. It was the least I could do."

"The least you could have done was not turn your back on all his father taught you. I suppose I shouldn't be surprised. Then again, who knows where we'd be today had I not allowed you to fraternize with those godless heathens?" She sighed and shook her head. "I had so hoped I raised you better, but I guess I failed you."

"If you see it that way, nothing I could say will change it." Abby shifted her purse off her shoulder and put it down at her feet. *Marlon was right, this thing weighs a ton.* No sooner did she let go of the straps than a black blur rocketed from it and into the nearby trees. "DOMINO!"

"Abigail Palmer!" Gladys' shocked voice was all too familiar. "How dare you bring that beast to a solemn occasion like this! For God's sake, what are you, seven?"

Abby didn't even look back as she chased after him. *How did he get in my purse in the first place?*

"Three guesses," said the dragon as he raced alongside her. "And the first two don't count."

Abby knew what that meant. "DOMINO!" She got about ten feet into the trees when the demon's laughter echoed in her ears. "YOU –"

"Oh relax, Abs," said Bjate. He appeared, leaning against a tree about two feet ahead of her. "Kitty cat's just fine." He pointed up to where, halfway up the tree, perched her terrified cat.

Her hands clenched at her sides and she glared at the demon. "There's no way he climbed up that high on his own."

"Nope, but then, if I hadn't snuck him along and pulled strings, you'd still be talking to that wannabe June Cleaver. So be a good girl and say thanks."

"Go to Hell." Abby kicked off her shoes and looked at the closest branches. She hadn't climbed a tree in years.

"I've been there, thank you, I found it quite lovely." Bjarte just grinned. "And if you're gonna try that, better take off your dress too."

"You wish."

"Abigail," said Aeneas, taking form beside her. "There is no need to climb up after him. It is a simple matter for me to –"

"Don't you dare!" Abby grabbed the nearest branch and hauled herself up into the tree. "You leave my cat alone, both of you! Where does it state he's fair game in your contracts anyway? I sure didn't sign up to have my pets used and abused like this. Back off!"

Bjarte held up his hands in mock surrender. "All right, won't touch the kitty again, promise."

"Abigail," said Dominic with a slight growl. "Don't be a fool. Get Little Wasp at least."

"And leave him here for Screwtape to play with?" She slipped slightly then pushed herself up another level. "When Satan's ice skatin'." It most likely didn't take as long as it seemed, but it felt like forever before she reached Domino. She tucked him under her arm and started back down. When she reached the second to last level, she carefully lowered the cat as far as she could and let him drop. *This was too easy...* Abby put her foot on the same branch she had used to climb up, only to hear a loud crack as it broke away.

"ABIGAIL!"

Her guardians' shouts echoed in her ears as she fell. A sharp pain went through her head when she hit the ground. Everything went black.

CHAPTER 27

"Hey, can I use your phone? Mine's dead as a doornail."

"Sorry pal, mine's out, too. I could have sworn I charged it."

Seriously, you couldn't use your car charger? Marlon walked over to where he had left his lady only to find her nowhere to be seen. "Abs? Abby!"

"Finally! You took your time, boy!"

"Hello, Mrs. Lynde." He fought to control his expression. *Not that you care what the old bat thinks of you.* "Where's Abby?"

"Off chasing her cat that she foolishly dragged to a funeral of all things!" The older woman thrust Abby's purse into his chest and walked past him. "The disrespect, I swear. The complete lack of common sense!"

Marlon slung the purse strap over his shoulder, shaking his head. *The real lack of common sense here is that you actually think Abs would do that.* He had no idea how the cat had gotten there, but as stupid as Gladys could be, she didn't usually lie. "Which way did she go?"

Gladys pointed the way without really looking before she stormed off.

He was almost to the trees when Domino shot out of them, ran to him with his tail humped over, and pawed at Marlon's pants. "Hey there, Dommy," Marlon said, reaching down and picking him up. "Bet you got your mom scared senseless." He looked to where the cat had come from. "And she should be right behind you."

Domino squirmed in Marlon's grip then bit down on his hand, forcing Marlon to drop him. The cat darted back into the trees, but didn't go more than a few feet in. He turned back and gave a sharp yowl, his fluffed tail lashing as he stared at Marlon.

You know she wouldn't just leave him on his own. Marlon felt a lump form in his throat as fear washed over him. He took a step forward and Domino raced off, forcing him to run. After what felt like forever, he spotted his lady on the ground... and standing over her was a dog-sized dragon.

The dragon snarled at a familiar-looking blond man, who stood there bowed over in laughter. In a heartbeat a second man appeared, staff in hand and struck at the blond, who pulled a sword to block him. The dragon's roar echoed in Marlon's ears.

What the Hell? Marlon shook his head and closed his eyes, and when he opened them the trio was gone. But Abby was still on the ground. He ran to her side, checking for a pulse. He found it, then pulled out his phone and swore. *I know I charged it!* He knew you were never supposed to move someone unconscious, but if he couldn't call a squad, he didn't have a choice. He took Abby in his arms and lifted her, carefully supporting her neck, and carried her back to the car. Domino was right behind him.

Abby first noticed the harsh smell of some kind of cleaner. Then she heard an annoying beeping and the faint scratching of a pencil on paper. She forced her eyes open, looked around and cringed. She hadn't been in a hospital room before, but she had seen them enough on her great-aunt's soap operas. The beeping sped up with her heart rate until she looked over and found Marlon in the chair beside her bed, furiously scratching at his sketch pad. "Mars-Bars?"

The pad dropped to the floor as his eyes locked on her face. "Oh, thank God!"

"What happened?" she asked, raising a hand to her aching head. She tried to force her memory to answer the question. The last thing she remembered was dropping Domino down from the tree. "Where's Dommy?" The beeping sped up again. *If Screwtape harmed my cat I'll...*

In answer, Marlon pulled a duffle bag off the floor beside him. He reached in, pulled out Domino, and put the black cat on her lap. "Looked like you fell out of a tree." He picked up his pad and started sketching again. "You've been out for a couple hours. How you feel?"

"Light-headed, mostly. My head hurts a bit." Abby hugged her cat tight and sighed. "Thank you for getting him. I still don't know how he ended up there." It was a miracle none of the staff had caught him sneaking the cat in.

"Mrs. Lynde thinks you brought him. Or that's what she said when she handed me your purse." Marlon kept his voice level but she could hear the frustration. "As if." He crumpled the paper and threw it at the trash can by the door before starting to scribble again. After a moment, he repeated the crumble-throw-start-over. "Damn it! I can't get this scene out of my head!"

Domino leaped out of her arms to catch the next sketch Marlon threw, snagging it midair, and Abby gently took it from him. She smoothed the paper out and her heart lodged in her throat.

"P.C.'s pretty talented, ain't he?" Bjarte's voice was amused. "Amazing how much detail he's got there."

The beeping sped up again with her heart rate and Abby clenched the blanket in her hands.

"Sorry, Abs. I swear I don't..." Marlon shook his head. "I must still have the game on the brain. Though the dragon don't look the same." He looked up at her, and whatever he saw on her face made concern wash over his. "Are you OK? Do I need to get the nurse?"

She couldn't wrap her head around it, but the evidence was staring up at her from the crumpled paper. "You saw them, too," she whispered. "You saw Dominic and..."

"Dominic?" Marlon repeated. "Wait, wasn't that your stuffed dragon? The one you asked your grandmother about?"

"You remember that?" Abby sighed. She picked up Domino and cradled him to her chest. "I... yes, yes it was. When I lost him, I pretended he was just invisible." Suspicion crept onto her face. "Grandma said that, actually. That he was just invisible now..."

"Abs... are you saying I saw your imaginary dragon?" Marlon sounded as shocked as she felt. "That's... that's not possible."

"Well, now you've gone and done it," said Bjarte, thankfully out of sight for the moment. "You gonna tell him you're crazy or what?"

"Shut up, Screwtape," snapped Dominic, rising up from the floor and putting his fore-paws on the bed. "She's far from insane."

He saw you, she thought at the dragon. *He SAW YOU. How is that possible?*

Aeneas answered, "In an effort to defend you from the deceiver, he summoned a great deal of power. Both the fools were expending so much energy they became tangible to the naked eye."

"Oh, we're the fools?" countered Nick. "Says the idiot that wasted precious time debating the morals of using her cat to get help. Little Wasp saw you, too, so get down off the high horse."

What should she say? How could she explain? *But he did see them...* She took a deep breath. "It... it would be... if he was just imaginary."

CHAPTER 28

"You aren't seriously considerin' that, are ya?" Bjarte's smug voice made her squeeze Domino so tightly he squeaked. "He'll just think you're nuts. And who knows? Maybe ya are."

No one asked you, Screwtape. Abby held up her hand to stop Marlon from speaking. "I know it sounds crazy. I *know* I used to think I was..." She put Domino back on her lap, then smoothed the paper again. *I have to come clean.* No relationship could be built on dishonesty, even if it was just by omission. And she'd been handed the chance to put all the cards on the table. "But then I learned otherwise the hard way. Because something imaginary can't wake you up when you fall asleep at the wheel."

Marlon's eyes narrowed at those words. He reached out and pulled the sketch to where they both could see it. He touched the dragon. "So if he's not imaginary, what is he?"

"This is gonna be fun," came the demon's commentary. "Go on, tell him how it's Grandpa's ghost hangin' around, and watch him bolt for the door if he don't call the white coats first."

She ignored him and tried to figure out how to explain. Her head still hurt, and she felt weird. Strangely, her thinking seemed perfectly clear. Like she understood everything about the trio right then, including why Aeneas had limits Bjarte didn't. Still, she could not have put it into words. "Two years ago, he was a mask."

"A mask for what?" Marlon's voice was calm. He was approaching this much as he had her grandfather's game. Analytical, precise, systematic. It was reassuring as much as worrying.

The beeping sped up again with her heart rate. *Just say it,* she told herself. *Just tell him. You have to tell him.* Tell him that her guardian angel and personal demon had used the dragon for years to play with her head. Tell him that now it was the guise for her grandfather's ghost. *It sounds insane and I live it.* She wrapped her arms around her cat, shivering.

He looked up, concern written all over his face. "You can tell me, Abs. You've never lied to me. You don't make stuff up..." He laid his hand on hers, careful not to dislodge her grip on her cat. "So... tell me."

So she did. She told him everything, from the near-wreck during her first driving exam to the showdown at Saint Pius X. She told him about the constant commentary, too. When she finished, Abby looked up at her best friend, heart lodged in her throat. *Please believe me. Please LET HIM believe me.*

Marlon reached out and touched the sketch again. He brushed his fingers over the dragon. "Dominic." Then the angel. "Aeneas." And lastly, the demon. "And his name is?"

Just say it, you have to! Her mouth felt dry and she coughed harshly. *Crap, come on Abby, just spit it out!*

Marlon reached for a half-filled water bottle in his duffle bag and handed it to her.

She took it gratefully and downed the rest. "His name is..."

Squeaking drew their attention to the white board by the door. One of the markers was writing apparently by itself. Block letters spelled out: IT'S BJARTE, P.C. The marker dropped back to the rack below the board like nothing happened.

Abby's blood ran cold, then fury flooded her veins. *How dare you!*

"C'mon," came the demon's smug voice. "Now he's gotta believe ya and ya didn't have to say my name either. Be a good girl and say thanks."

"P.C.?" Marlon repeated, his expression torn between shock and confusion.

"Prince Charming," Abby bit out, hugging Domino so tight he gave a sharp meow. She let go and clutched at the blankets. "He calls you Prince Charming!"

They both jumped as the door to her room opened.

Marlon grabbed Domino and shoved him into a duffle bag, then slung the bag over his shoulder. He reached out and squeezed her hand as a nurse came in, followed by his parents.

"Are you OK, dear?" the nurse asked, sending a glare at Marlon. "Your heart monitor went off a few times. He's not upsetting you is he?"

"He's fine," Abby said, glancing down at the sketch. "We were just talking..."

"I'll be back, Abs," said Marlon. His eyes darted to the bag. "I need to stretch my legs and take care of a few things." He squeezed her hand again and bolted out the door.

Wendel watched his son go, then shook his head. "You'd think the Hounds of Hell were on his heels." His concerned gaze turned to her. "How you feeling, Abby?"

She went over the same answers she had already given Marlon, but her mind was on her boyfriend, not his family. Her eyes went to The Dragon sitting beside her bed. *Please?*

Dominic sighed and nodded. He took off out the door Marlon had left open. "I'll see what he's up to. Don't worry about it. Little Wasp's stronger than you think."

*

Marlon put Domino back in his carrier and turned the heat on in the car. *Last thing I need is to get kicked out over her cat.* He sat in the seat beside Domino, one hand stroking him through the door. *Thank God Abby's crazy prepared.* He had laughed when she put the foldable carrier in the trunk despite having a plastic one in her apartment. *Are you going to keep going over everything but what just happened? Are you really that foolish?*

I can't. I can't just... what the Hell just happened? This can't be some candid camera prank show. He played back watching that marker write all on its own. Sure, he had always assumed that there was more to life than what met the eye, but to see it firsthand... *And Abs has lived with this knowledge for two years now... alone.* He couldn't stay where he was. Every instinct yelled at him to get back to his lady. He shut off the car and draped a blanket from the back seat over the carrier. He made sure to crack the windows before walking back to the front door.

Are you just going to walk in and act like nothing happened? The little voice in the back of his head sounded harsh. *You know, everything's changed. You can't just go back to the way things were. You're an idiot if you think that.*

Marlon took a deep breath and started walking down the sidewalk around the hospital. He needed time to think. There was no way he could deal with his family, never mind Abby right now. His whole world had turned upside down. He ended up in front of a statue of the Blessed Mother and stared up at her. *Mother Mary, pray for me...* He chuckled sadly. *No, pray for Abby. She needs you more than I do.*

Why had Bjarte pulled that stunt? What had he hoped to accomplish? Wouldn't letting him doubt her story have served him better? What would be gained by...? *You have lived your whole life unaccepting of the supernatural. It stands to reason that proof of its existence would send you running.*

Anger had him shaking. "Run away?" he asked aloud. "Abandon Abs? *Like Hell!*" He glared up at the sky, then looked around him. It was getting dark, the parking lot's lights were coming on. "If you're listening, you bastard, you better get one thing straight: Abby's mine. My friend, my lady, my everything. And you mess with her, you mess with me. You touch her again, trust me, I'll find a way to send your ass straight back where it belongs!"

The lights flickered and one near him went out before he heard a voice *right* beside him say: "Well said, Little Wasp. I'll hold you to that."

CHAPTER 29

Marlon walked back to Abby's room, hands stuffed in his pockets and his mind going a mile a minute. His heart felt like it would fly out of his chest, but no one seemed to notice. He heard raised voices as he approached her door and almost walked into his father. "What's going on?"

"She's cleared for release," replied Wendel as he held the door open for his wife. "But she's insisting she can go home alone, and the doctor's adamant that someone needs to be with her."

"So where are you going?" Marlon rocked back on his heels, grateful for the distraction. *She's sure not going to be left alone on my watch. Not with the real Mr. Creepy running around.*

"Home to get the cot Dad uses out of the garage, and to make up the couch. You'll end up at her place on the cot or ours on the couch, no doubt, so might as well be prepared."

"Yeah, well, I doubt there will be any sensational news," added Datura, shaking her head. "Good luck, son. You'll need it." As she walked away she muttered, "Why do you all pick such stubborn ladies?"

"Because then life's not boring," replied Wendel.

Then Marlon stood alone in the hall and he braced himself before pushing open the door. "Is everything OK in here?"

"Everything is *fine*," Abby replied through her teeth. "I'm alive, I'm awake, and I'm perfectly capable of going home."

The doctor took off his glasses and cleaned them on his jacket. "Miss Palmer, we've been over this. You have a concussion. You need rest, and at least for tonight, need someone watching to make sure you don't show any symptoms later. I cannot in good faith send you home without knowing someone will be with you."

"I. Am. Fine." Abby's eyes darted to the floor beside him, then back to the doctor. "I'll sign a waiver. Just let me go home! I have school tomorrow!"

"Miss Palmer, I've already written an excuse. Mrs. Samson will call the school for you tomorrow. You need rest, both physically and mentally. That means you need to take a few days off for –"

"I am fine!"

Uh, I don't think so, Abs. Marlon knew she had a temper, but he'd never thought she could be this irrational. "That's not going to be a problem, sir. I'll stay the night with her. No big deal."

The doctor raised a brow. "And you are?"

"Her boyfriend," Marlon replied.

"Hmm." Disapproval was written all over the doctor's face. Considering the guy looked his grandfather's age, that wasn't too surprising. The fact the automatic assumption had been that he was responsible for Abby's stay still chafed.

"Marlon, you can't stay with me it's not –"

"You can go home to your own place, and I'll crash on Grandpa's cot," he replied calmly. "Or we'll go to my folks', and I'll crash on the couch. Up to you." He glanced at the doctor. "But either way, you ain't going home by yourself."

"The Hell I'm not!" Abby glared at him. "Marlon Samson! Don't you start acting like some stalker-control freak romance novel hero!"

"Miss Palmer, he is being reasonable," replied the doctor. "Which is more than I can say for you. I hope this is the concussion talking. Thank you, sir, I'll send up a wheelchair." He dropped his clipboard in the pocket on the door and shut it behind him.

Marlon fought the urge to step back when Abby met his gaze. In an effort to diffuse the tension, he asked, "So how long has your guardian angel called me 'Little Wasp'?"

She blinked, then looked down at the floor beside her bed before laughing so hard the bed shook. She stopped short and put a hand to her head. "OK, laughing is bad." She looked up and smiled. "Aeneas doesn't call you that. Dom... Grandpa Nick does."

He sat straight down on the floor and put his head in his hands. "That was... that was The Dragon?"

"Keep your voice down," she hissed. "Trust me, you don't want to see a shrink."

Marlon held up his hand. "Abs... give me a minute here. Cause... I was just outside and I swear I heard –"

"– Grandpa Nick tell you he'd hold you to whatever it was you said," she finished, shaking her head before putting it in her hands. "OK, sudden movements are bad, too."

You are going to look very responsible sitting on the floor when they come in with the wheelchair. Marlon took several deep breaths as he tried to process everything he had seen and heard. He didn't do drugs so he knew he wasn't hallucinating. "So wait, he told you what I said?"

"He told me you're 'a lot like Wasp, and Screwtape's an idiot to think he can run you off,' quote unquote." Abby rested her chin in her hand. "Why? Did you say something stupid?"

Marlon's face turned red and he bolted to his feet as the door opened. *Thank God...* he stopped himself. *This is going to take some getting used to.* He stepped aside so the nurse could help his lady into the wheelchair. *You seem to be doing quite well actually.* He shook his head at the thought and followed the nurse downstairs.

CHAPTER 30

"You can go home now."

"Nope."

"Mars-Bars..."

"Staying."

"MARLON!"

"Why don't you ask The Dragon if he thinks you should be alone?"

"That's not the point!"

"Then what is?"

Abby started at Marlon, fighting the urge to pull her hair out. As it was, the two pills she'd taken hadn't kicked in yet, so making her head hurt worse didn't sound reasonable. Then again, neither did sharing a room with her boyfriend. "Marlon, do you remember Halloween?"

Marlon looked confused. Then he rolled his eyes as he put Domino on her lap. "Abs, seriously. You have a head injury. If you think I'm gonna take advantage of that, you're crazy."

"Very funny," she replied, scooping her cat into her arms. "Still, one room plus hormones doesn't equal anything good."

"Aw, come on." Bjarte laughed, still out of sight. "Any guy his age has rubbers on him, and the release would distract ya from the headache."

She gritted her teeth and flinched when Domino yowled due to her grip. "Sorry, sweetheart." She scratched his ears. "It's OK."

"What'd Mr. Creepy say now?" Marlon looked around the room as he sat on the side of her bed. "Already told you to knock it off, creep. Believe me with Dad's connections I can find out how to send you on a one-way ticket home real fast."

The demon's laughter echoed in her ears and she looked over to see him appear, bent over in amusement a few feet away. "That I'd like to see, considerin' that would be rippin' me from my assignment."

Domino pulled out of her arms and stalked to the end of the bed. He growled, his fur standing on end and his tail lashing like a whip.

The demon taunted in sing-song, "Kitty Kitty's in a tizzy."

Marlon calmly flipped his grandfather's favorite gesture in the direction Domino was facing, then reached out and stroked the cat. "Good boy."

"It doesn't work that way," Abby said, lying back into her pillows. "I already tried to run him off, and all I got was six-months' peace." She sighed. "I'm 'his charge' just as much as I'm Aeneas'. So I'm stuck with him."

"I call bull," Marlon replied. "You wouldn't be the only person stuck with a duo like this then."

Abby spoke before one of her trio could chime in. "Everyone else does have them; they just don't hear them like I do." She closed her eyes. "I'm the idiot that hung on to my imaginary friend too long." *How did you explain that again?*

"Everyone hears the voices," replied Aeneas. "It is just as they grow older, they sound more and more like themselves."

She repeated that, and waited for the freak out. "You're taking this surprisingly well."

"Well, what else am I supposed to do? I can't deny what I saw and heard. That would be stupid. So, I'll adjust." She felt him pat her knee. "I just wish I'd known sooner. Sucks you had to deal with this alone."

"You're too good to be true," she replied. *If my head didn't hurt I'd assume I was dreaming this.* "Seriously, Mars-Bars. You need to go home."

"Don't start that again. If you honestly think I can't control myself, Abs, you kinda need to rethink every time we've been alone together since your birthday two years ago."

Her face got so hot, she hoped it was only emotion and not a symptom of her concussion. She didn't dare open her eyes to see his expression. When he laid his hand on her forehead, it felt cold in comparison. She felt him get up, heard water run and shut off, and then felt a cool cloth press against her forehead.

"I'm here, Abs, and I'm not going anywhere. Come Hell or high water."

"Aw, is that a crack in the Prince's shining armor I hear?"

Go to Hell, Screwtape. The cool of the cloth went a long way to soothing her headache, but she kept her eyes tightly closed. She had heard it too. And knowing Marlon, he wouldn't break down in front of her. So she gave him what privacy she could. "I know, Mars-Bars."

"So... uh." He started playing with her hair, and she fought not to slap his hand away. "How... you don't know how to tell when the voices aren't... yours, do you?"

"Looks like Little Wasp's been hearing voices, too." Dominic chuckled. "At least he's better prepared now."

"Marlon, please... don't touch my hair right now, it just makes my head hurt." Abby winced at how fast he took his hand away. "Deceivers are... they..."

"We'll talk about it some other time. You're supposed to be resting anyway." The bed flexed as he got up. A click and sudden soothing darkness told her he'd shut the light off. "Try and relax, OK? I'm right here if you need me." She heard the squeak of the cot as he laid down. "Night, Abs."

"Night, Mars-Bars." She reached out and stroked Domino as he curled up beside her, and drifted off to his motorboat purring.

Insane laughter echoed off the cave walls, and Abby felt the rough rock tear the flesh off her bare feet. There was nowhere to run, nowhere to go. You can get out the same way you came in. But where had she came in? She had no memory of how she'd gotten there. There was no light to even see where she was, but instinctively she recognized the dragon's cave. The laughter came again, and she knew she wasn't alone. *Dommy!* She called out for The Dragon, for Aeneas, but no response came. Only the demon's laughter.

"I doubt Kitty will be a lot of help right now." His voice was far too smug. As if he had already won. "But I can get him for you if you want."

ASHLEIGH D.J. CUTLER

"You leave my cat alone, you —" she surprised herself with her word choice that followed. One hand ran along the jagged rock wall, and she started to move sideways, hoping to find an exit.

"OK, not the kitty then." The voice seemed to come from everywhere at once. "Maybe... hmm, parents are already gone... grandpa... and you don't care about your aunt..."

Aeneas! Dominic! It was obvious he could hear her thoughts, but she didn't want to disorient herself further. *Grandpa Nick!*

"Oh, I know."

She heard fingers snap.

"Maybe that cocky Prince of yours. I mean it takes some nerve to flip me off, don't you think? Maybe need to teach him his place."

Her heart lodged in her throat. "You leave Marlon alone! He's not yours!"

"No..." Flames abruptly filled the cave, and even when she closed her eyes against the glow she could still feel the heat. He laughed when she shrieked. "But you are, aren't you, Dragonfly?"

"NO! NO! I'M NOT!" She pressed against the wall as the flames licked her clothes. "NO!"

"Abs!"

Marlon's fearful voice had her heart racing. *No, no! Leave him alone!*
"ABBY!"

"Abs, come on, wake up!" Marlon was reluctant to shake her too hard, but if she didn't snap out of it soon he was going to dump the glass of cold water he'd just filled on her. The whimpers she made cut him to the quick. "ABBY!"

"Marlon, get ou —" She sat up in an instant, cutting herself off as she saw him sitting there, his forehead wrinkled with worry. "Oh, it was just a dream."

He watched as she fought to catch her breath, repeating "only a dream" over and over again. She rubbed her eyes. "Abs... are you OK?" Out of the blue, he remembered her telling him that she'd been having bad dreams when she'd looked, as he put it, like a vampire. *Which was pretty close to when she went AWOL on me.*

"Fine, Mars-Bars." She rubbed her head. "Where's the pain pills? Ow..."

He reached over and got the bottle from the nightstand. He handed her two pills and the glass of water he had sat down before he noticed her distress. He waited until she'd swallowed them. "Nightmare? Mr. Creepy playing games, maybe?"

She still choked on the water and coughed for a moment before she cleared her throat. "You are too smart for your own good." She sighed. "He does that. It's no big deal, Mars-Bars." She sounded so tired he didn't have the heart to argue. "I'm going back to sleep, OK? It'll be OK."

"Sure, Abs." He pulled the comforter back around her and turned the lamp off. Then he climbed onto the bed beside her, pulling her spare blanket off the trunk and tucking it around them both.

"Mar-lon," she hissed. "You are not —"

"You start having another nightmare, I'm waking you up as soon as possible." He forced his voice to mimic his elders' when they closed a subject. "Nothing's gonna happen with four layers of cloth between us, so just relax. Love you, Abs."

"Love you, too, Mars-Bars..." After a moment she whispered, "I swear the stubbornness is inherited."

CHAPTER 31

"So..." said Marlon the next morning as they sat down to breakfast. "What are 'deceivers'? I mean..." He dipped his head when she said grace, then cut into his pancakes. "How... how do you tell it's them and not you?"

Abby took a bite, then took her time chewing as she tried to think of an answer. She was so used to dealing with her duo now. She thought back to when they shared the mask. "They're... They're your doubts. Your fears. That little voice inside that says, 'go head, no one will ever know.' That says, 'you deserve it, go on.' And before you ask, guardians do the opposite. Your guardian is basically your conscience."

"Guess we know where they got that 'good angel, bad angel' shoulder stuff from."

"Maybe."

The rest of the meal was spent in silence, as each was lost in their own thoughts. After the dishes were cleared away, Abby asked, "So how are you going to get ready for school? Did your parents leave you a change of clothes?"

"Yeah, but I'm not going to school." Marlon filled the sink and started on the dishes. "And don't give me a lecture. You're out for three days, so I'll be sticking around until then. Felice will bring our homework by later."

"You're doing it again."

"Doing what?"

"The white knight thing. And bordering on control freak."

162

Marlon turned around and raised an eyebrow. "Abs. You. Have. A. Head injury. It's not like you have a paper cut and I'm ready to rush you to the hospital. I'm treating this seriously because it is serious." He turned and went back to the dishes. He watched her out of the corner of his eye.

Abby rubbed at her temples before retreating back to her bed. "I'm just going to lay down all day. There's no reason for you to miss school." She sighed and closed her eyes, snuggling into her pillow. "You can't tell me you're excused."

"Family emergency. Dad already took care of it." He put the last dish away, then got out the cat food for Domino. He scratched the cat's ears as he ate. "There you go, buddy."

"What are you going to do all day, watch me sleep?"

"That'd be creepy." Marlon got the cot and sat it down beside the bed before lying down himself. "Probably crash, too, but I'll be here just in case Mr. Creepy tries anything again."

Abby flinched. "You realize he and the guy in the game aren't one and the same?"

"Yeah, but the name seems to bug you, and Screwtape is almost a compliment." Marlon folded his arms behind his head, squirming to get off the pipes supporting the canvas. Was *more comfortable in the bed.* But he wasn't about to suggest it. Though waking up beside her had been nice. *I could get used to that.* "Why is the name such a big deal anyway?"

Abby didn't answer for so long he was sure she'd already fallen asleep. Then she said, "I.... Names give power. Naming something... it can... I'm..." She huffed. "Thanks, I didn't really want him to know that. I don't say his name because I'm scared it'll give him a power boost."

"Fear of a name only increases fear of the thing itself," he quoted, only for her to snort.

"Yeah, he said that, right before he knocked me straight out of my chair to the floor." She groaned. "Great, hitting my head disabled the brain-to-mouth filter."

Marlon bit his tongue. *She didn't tell you before because you wouldn't have believed it. Don't jump down her throat now.* "Abs... did he *make you* fall out of the tree?"

"Yes. He used Domino the same way he did Troubadour." Her voice caught and he had to fight the urge to get up and hug her. "If I had any sense, I wouldn't have a cat."

"Used Troubadour?" he repeated, then wanted to smack himself. He knew all too well that the cords chewed by her cat had started the fire that killed her parents. He swore.

"Pretty much. He decided to gloat about it a while back."

Marlon quickly changed his mind about sharing the bed. If he had been beside her, he wouldn't have been able to hide how fast his heart was beating. *There's nothing you can do about it, so there's no sense in worrying about it.* He rolled his eyes. *Like that's gonna stop me. Besides, I can do something...* "Dad would know how to kick a demon to the curb." He didn't realize he'd said the last out loud until Abby replied.

"You can't. I already explained this. I'm stuck with him... just like you're stuck with yours."

"About that..." Marlon swallowed hard. "It's just... you sure there's not a way to know for sure which voice in your head is which?" *You really like asking stupid questions, don't you? If it was that simple, it would be common knowledge.*

"Mars-Bars." It came out both fond and exasperated. "I've gone over all this a hundred times myself. It doesn't do any good. All you can do is live your life and hope you don't screw up." She turned over, her back to him. "Now, either go to school or go to sleep please. My head already hurts enough without going in circles."

"Sure, Abs." He turned over himself, trying to get comfortable. "Sorry." He lay there awake long after her breathing told him she had drifted off. *There's got to be a way to fight this.*

That's what you think.

CHAPTER 32

"I'm fine."

"Abs..."

"Marlon, it's been three days." She rubbed her temples. *"And we've almost been at each other's throats twice today. This apartment isn't made for two people. Look, just... get out for a bit, OK? Get some fresh air, a change of scenery... please."*

"What about you? You've been cooped up in here too and —"

"And I have homework to finish. I'll be fine." She looked him dead in the eye. *"If it's You-Know-Who you're worried about, I've dealt with him my whole life."*

"But... But..." It was useless. *"OK, OK, but... call me if anything —"*

"If anything comes up. I need anything. I feel weird. I know, I know. Go!"

"Yes, ma'am."

Marlon rode around town on his bike, wondering how much time he'd have to kill before Abby would feel they'd had enough of a break. Yes, the apartment was a bit... close. But he didn't like leaving her when he wasn't sure she was healed. *You realize the only thing that's changed is you're aware of the situation? So why are you worrying so much? She's survived this long, you know.* He stopped at a red light. *Yeah, but there's always that chance. He's come close twice now... third time's the charm.*

And there's nothing you could do anyway.

I don't like having something I can't fight! The light turned green and he realized he was headed home. *I need to talk to someone... maybe Dad will...* He sighed. *No, that won't work. I tell him The Dragon's hanging around, he'll freak seven ways from Sunday. And The Dragon's lady's out. She'd think I was just making it up. I need an expert in these things.*

An expert in demons, this day and age? Yeah, right. What are you going to do, talk to an exorcist? Be serious.

Maybe not an exorcist... Marlon turned onto Main Street and pushed

166

the bike to the speed limit. *But a priest might not be a bad idea.*

Oh, come on! You don't even believe in that crap!

Can't meet the Devil and not believe in God, he thought, then stopped short at an intersection. His eyes narrowed. *"It's your doubts, your fears...." You know what, I sure am doing this. Abs thought going there was the right idea, and...*

And you are being completely foolish!

Am I really... Screwtape? He laughed at the sudden silence. No doubts, no second-guesses. Then...

You are smarter than many give you credit for.

Marlon shook his head and took off for Reynoldsburg and Waggoner Road. The sooner he spoke with a priest the better, and he didn't need the gossips at Abby's current church running their mouths. *But I do need answers.*

St. Pius X, Abby's childhood church, was easily the most intimidating place he had ever been. The white supports and stone walls with the pitch-black roof always made him think of a final dungeon in a video game. Not that Marlon would have ever told Abby as much. He went around the back and parked his bike, then tried to decide if he was better off going inside or trying the priests' place. *Rectory, Marlon, he thought, it's called a rectory.*

You actually think this will do anything? At most you'll be laughed out of the office.

He sighed as he pocketed his keys. *No wonder Ab's is a grouch sometimes.* He walked over to the rectory and knocked on the door. After a few minutes, he tried again. Nothing. *Must be blessing the holy water...* He stood there, hands in his pockets, and looked over at the church. *What is it about this place that made Abby think it would tip the odds in her favor?*

It didn't. If anything, it escalated the issue.

Sooo... Marlon thought, *me going in won't make a difference either, right?* He matched words to action and regretted it the second he stepped into the dark vestibule. *This place feels almost... haunted.* Goosebumps covered his arms and the hair stood up on the back of his neck.

His heart pounded in his chest as he jerked the doors open, not even caring how much he must look like a fool to Drew. The words, "Please keep her safe, let her be safe!" repeating in his head. The dark entryway disoriented him for a minute, then he saw pews through the stained glass and...

STOP IT! He forced the flashback aside. The apprehension was harder to shake.

Get out! You don't belong here!

No, he thought firmly. *I've been here before, when Abs finished off the sacraments.* Still, he all but ran across the entryway to the sanctuary. He pulled the door open, and, leaving the holy water untouched, stepped inside. The unease only increased as the door closed behind him. He looked toward the altar, feeling like a child about to be caught sneaking in the teacher's lounge.

Looking around everywhere. Too much to take in. Bright light pouring through the windows and the skylight in the corner. He tried to stop the memories, but it was like someone else was playing back his files. *The smell of incense. Sandalwood. Abby's favorite... Where's it coming from? Stepping further in and spotting Abby on the ground by what he would learn was called the tabernacle. Running, then tripping and skinning his knee because of the dip in the floor.*

Marlon didn't trip this time as he slowly walked down the main aisle in the center of the room. He passed the altar, and took the few steps to the rise before the tabernacle. He genuflected before he made the Sign of the Cross. *Up, down, left, right...* Abby had taught him that.

"ABBY! ABS!" Ignoring the pain, jumping the steps to get beside her. Shaking her shoulders. Noticing the light fading... Must've been clouds or something. Relief when she opened her eyes, confusion when she wouldn't answer him directly. More confusion when she looked even more distracted than she had before.

"And now I know why," he said aloud. "She'd just fought off a demon." *Right here, right where I am, she unmasked the dragon...* The unease he had felt since stepping inside nagged at his senses, demanding to be recognized. "WHAT DO YOU WANT?"

You don't belong here, the voice hissed again. *You are mocking true believers with your stance and your gestures. You'll just get Him angry with you.*

If He really gives a crap about a handful of gestures and not what's in here... Marlon laid his hand over his heart, much like Abby had when he'd missed Mass. *I'd be really surprised.* He turned his eyes on the wooden Ascending Jesus figure attached to the center of the wall behind the altar. *If she's under attack, then she is doing something right, I'd say.* He shook his head and stood up. He reached out, touching the stone wall beside the tabernacle. Then he turned around and headed out of the church. *Abby didn't go to a priest... so...*

Human rituals are not going to change anything here. Human faith, on the other hand... human trust... just might.

Oh, so you're finally going to offer some advice? Marlon pulled his keys from his pocket. He looked at his watch. It had barely been an hour. *Good. So what do I do, oh wise angel?*

Trust yourself, and trust her.

CHAPTER 33

"You can't keep popping those like that," Dominic protested. "You'll give yourself an ulcer."

"This is my second set, and I can take eight total a day." Abby rubbed her head and eyes, wishing she could lay down. She laid another assignment in her "done" tray and started the next, despite how hard she had to strain to keep her vision focused properly.

"You *should* lay down. If Little Wasp was here he'd –"

"He's not here, and that's why I have to get this done." She looked at the clock and sighed. *It's barely been an hour? Crap.* She looked at the phone on the desk beside her. *I wonder if Bryan would do me a favor?*

"Abigail, for Pete's sake!" Dominic growled from his place beside her. "You are a grown woman. You don't need someone else to run interference for you with your boyfriend!"

"Tell that to the white knight that thinks he can fight a demon." The laptop messenger dinged and she sighed. "I swear if that's Mars-Bars..."

RaspberryRaposa: Hey Dragonfly! What's up? Heard you forgot to land on your feet the other day. Doing OK?

DragonflyGirl: Doing homework, but yeah, I did fall out of a tree. Random tell you?

RaspberryRaposa: Yep! And we spun the wheel to see who got to talk to you first, since he said not to overwhelm ya, that ya can't handle lots of crap all at once right now. I won!

Abby drilled her fingers on her desk. *He means well, he's just trying to help...*

"Help himself into your pants, maybe."

"Damn you straight to Hell, Screwtape!" She looked around, expecting the demon to show himself for laughs. "This is all your fault! I had him almost calmed down, then you pull your stupid stunt and now he's acting like I'm made of glass!"

"No one said you had to climb up after Kitty. You could have called Prince Charming to do it."

She shoved herself away from the desk and stood up. "Oh, and given you the chance to hurt someone *else* that means something to me?" She forced her voice back down, and chose her words with purpose. "In your dreams... *Bjarte*. In. Your. Dreams."

"Whoo-hoo!" The demon appeared by the door, laughing. "You finally grew a pair. Good for you!" He clapped sarcastically. "Now what? Gonna get out the sandalwood again? It didn't work before, won't now."

Maybe it was the lingering headache. Maybe it was the pain meds dulling her mind. It didn't matter. Right then, she realized the one thing she hadn't done since she sent him packing two years before. It might have not been for good, but it had given her a break, and even that was worth it. "In the name of the Father, the Son and the Holy Spirit... BE GONE!" She clenched her fists and glared at him. "And if that's not good enough for you, I'm sure *Annie* and Grandpa Nick will be happy to show you the door!"

"You don't really mean that." Bjarte narrowed his eyes. "All it's gonna do is tick me off, and I'll take it out on you... or maybe that boytoy of yours. I took out your dear gramps, your parents... what makes you think he's safe?"

She started shaking – from anger or fear, she couldn't say. "The fact that you are a liar."

"Even a liar speaks the truth sometimes." Bjarte folded his arms and smirked. "You gonna take the chance this ain't one of them?"

"Abigail..." Aeneas appeared beside her, then his staff appeared in his hand. "Has it occurred to you just why he objects so much to your relationship with the boy?"

"Marlon," she corrected. "Little Wasp. Either or, he has a name. Use it."

"Very well. Marlon." Aeneas kept his eyes on Bjarte. "What allowed him to be driven off was more than just your requesting aid, though that was part of it. It was the fact an extremely honest request for your protection was being asked at the same time."

The fury on Bjarte's face gave proof to his statement.

Abby froze completely. "*Marlon* tipped the scales? *MARLON?*"

"Little Wasp didn't even believe in the Man Upstairs, and he begged and bargained with Him. That's called love." Dominic growled, his tail swinging to his sides. "It's why Screwtape's been trying to get you upset enough to break it off. 'Cause if ya do...."

"Then Marlon wouldn't care anymore." Abby clenched her fists and crossed the distance until she stood almost toe-to-toe with Bjarte. "You understand nothing." She looked him straight in the eye. "Marlon *loves* me. I *love* him."

"He drives you crazy. Not that you weren't already."

"I drive him crazy, too. But would he be there if I needed him, even if I completely ticked him off? Yes. Would I go to him if he needed me, even if I was ready to strangle him last time I saw him? Yes. Because love isn't just playing house. It's being there for the other person, doing what's right for *them*, even if it hurts *you*." She narrowed her eyes. "Which you clearly can't comprehend, now or ever." She heard the messenger's ding and turned her back on him. "You know what? I'm not afraid of you. I feel sorry for you... but I'm not afraid of you!"

"Looks like I'm not the only liar, then."

Abby ignored him, sitting back down. She facepalmed at the fact she'd been so caught up in her argument with the demon she'd apparently missed more than just one message.

RaspberryRaposa: Hey, you still there?

RaspberryRaposa: Ava? Dragonfly? Hey... uh look don't blame Random. Head injuries are no laughing matter...

RaspberryRaposa: Look, you reply or I'm calling Random. I'm not getting yelled at cause ya passed out talking to me and I didn't do anything!

DragonflyGirl: Sorry, had to do something real quick. So you won, huh? Talking to me's a prize? *laughs* So you all been OK?

RaspberryRaposa: Geez, don't do that, something happens to you on my watch Random will have my head. Anyway, yeah we're good. Still need a bigger cat population around, but right now you likely couldn't keep your head in the game.

DragonflyGirl: Most likely not. I've got to get my homework done before Random gets back and puts me on bed rest again. I'll try and catch up with ya'll later, OK?

RaspberryRaposa: You got it, I'll pass the word on. Take it easy.

Abby smiled then started back on her homework, only to turn to find Bjarte standing right beside her. She shrugged, ignoring his glare. "Got something else stupid to say?"

"Enjoy the peace while it lasts. I play for keeps, too."

CHAPTER 34

Marlon walked into the bedroom he shared with his brothers to find Kenny sitting in a chair, reading. His legs were propped up on a cardboard box and Isaac was nowhere in sight. "Lemme guess. He's in the box, isn't he?"

"HELP ME!" cried Isaac, his voice muffled. "I didn't do nothing! I swear!"

"How'd ya guess?" Kenny turned the page, not even bothering to respond to their younger brother's words. "So you and Abby living in sin now or what?"

Marlon walked over and sat down on the bed, stretching his legs out so they rested on the box beside Kenny's. "I'm sure you didn't do nothing, Ike. Otherwise you wouldn't be there."

"That a yes?" Kenny continued reading his book, ignoring Isaac's protests. "'Cause I'll help ya pack up your stuff if you're moving out."

"I'm not moving out... though when I do, you'll be the first to know." He pressed his feet down harder on the shaking box. "So, what's new around here?"

"You got mail." Kenny jerked a thumb over at the nightstand. "Looks pretty official and stuff, if you ask me. Hope you don't have jury duty or something."

"You better let the brat out before Mom comes in." Marlon got up and flopped on his bed, grabbing the letter. He saw the return address and blinked. *Wait, why would the contest people be sending snail mail?* He opened the letter and began to read. *"We regret to inform you that your entry didn't place, but that is not to say it is a poor game. It simply is*

174

too overtly moralistic for our company. If you would be willing to make the following changes, we would like to make an offer to distribute Path of the Dragon." His mouth went dry as he scanned the list. *Abs will never stand for this. It wouldn't be The Dragon's game anymore.*

Yeah, but she wants it out right? Sometimes you gotta make sacrifices.

Marlon folded the letter up and stuffed it in his pocket. He glanced at the clock and sighed. *Only been two hours. Crap. Might as well get some rest...* He had just closed his eyes when a weight dropped on his stomach. "OW! Hey, what gives?"

"Thank you, Marlon!" Isaac was sitting on Marlon's middle, grinning. "Wanna play?"

"You said to let him out," Kenny said, shaking his head as he turned another page. "So this is all on you, bro."

*

Abby paced. Her homework was done, the minor cleaning she could pull off was done, she'd taken a small nap, and it was starting to get dark. Marlon wasn't back yet. *He's not going to be gone all night...* She glanced at the phone, then at the laptop. *Right?*

"You wanted him to go back to school," Dominic reminded her. "And if there's one thing a Samson does, it's –"

"Will you stop with the 'a Samson does this' crap?" She sighed and put a hand to her forehead. *Great, the headache's coming back.* "Marlon's Marlon. He's not Bryan or Wendel."

Dominic rolled his eyes, laying his head upon his fore-paws. "Maybe not, but name one time I've been wrong."

In answer, Abby held up her wrist with the charm bracelet. "Right or not, stop it." She took a deep breath. "Please. Grandpa Nick. He's not just your best friend's grandson, OK? Seriously, how much am I like Mom?"

"More than you think." Dominic's tail tapped against the bed. "Her and Cowboy. The mix is what makes you, you. Same with Little Wasp."

"So, nothing about me comes from you?" She smiled. "Is that what you're saying?" There was a knock on the door and she almost tripped getting to it. Common sense pulled her up short and she asked, "Who is it?"

"Just me, Abs." Marlon's voice sounded slightly strained. "I know you think I should stay home and head back to school, but I got some mail and... well, I've got some news I wanna talk about in person. Can I come in?"

She unlocked the door and gave him a smile. "I don't know, can you?"

Marlon rolled his eyes as he stepped past her. "Very funny." He sat down at her table and pulled out a letter. "You might want to sit down."

She obliged. "I know your family didn't say anything about us staying together unattended in a one-room apartment. So what's got you so..." She couldn't think of the word.

"I heard back from the contest." Marlon drew a letter out of his pocket and slid it across to her. "The Dragon's game didn't make the cut. But... if some changes are made, they'd take it on anyway." He glanced around the room. "Thing is. Those changes..."

"He's on the bed," she told him as she scanned the letter. "These changes would completely change the point of the game."

"I know." Marlon folded his arms and rested his head on his hands. "Sorry, Abs. We'll have to keep looking. There's got to be someone who'll take it, storyline intact."

"I'm not surprised." Dominic jumped down off the bed and sat beside them. "I pretty much got laughed out of the office for the same reason. A religious-themed game just doesn't catch people's eye. Tell Little Wasp thanks for trying."

Abby rolled her eyes, but did pass on the message. "Maybe I need to invest in an Ouija board."

"NO!"

Flinching at the internal shout, she put her head in her hands. "Guys, drop the volume please. I still have a headache." She closed her eyes. "The idiots can't take a joke."

Marlon smiled, reaching out and rubbing her head softly. "I take it angel and dragon don't like the idea?" He chuckled. "They've got a point. How'd I know which was talking?"

"Exactly!" Aeneas tsked. "At least the boy has that much sense. It might not even be us conversing with him."

"Yeah, that'd be fun," chimed in Bjarte. "Could tell Prince Charming all about your petty complaints and crap. See how long he sticks around then."

"Did you try this hard to get Bryan away from Grandpa Nick?" Abby blinked when she realized she had asked the question aloud. "Uh, I mean...."

"You mean Mr. Creepy don't like me hanging around." Marlon's face screwed up in annoyance. "Good, 'cause I don't like him doing it either. We're even."

"Bjarte. His name's Bjarte. And *his*," she added, jerking her thumb at her boyfriend, "is Marlon. Not Prince Charming, not 'the boy.' Marlon. Use it."

The demon's laughter echoed in her ears. "Whatever you say, Dragonfly."

CHAPTER 35

"I'm surprised to see you back, Abby."

"Mel, please." Abby slid her tray along as they moved with the rest of the lunch line. "I don't want to have to go to the nurse's office to get more Tylenol." She sighed. "School policy on pills sucks sometimes."

"I was just going to say as much as Marlon fusses over you, I didn't expect you back for at least a week." Melissa picked up her tray and followed Abby and Felice to their usual table where Marlon was waiting. "Still, if I could quit hearing how you 'disrespectfully brought your cat' to my father-in-law's funeral, it'd be nice."

"Mrs. Lynde needs to get off her high horse," remarked Felice. "Her and your mother-in-law. Why are they so dang nosy?"

"No idea." Melissa sat down and opened her can of lemonade. "If they actually think Abby'd be that stupid, *they* need the shrink."

"Thanks for the vote of confidence." Abby put her tray down and pulled out her chair. She went to sit down, only to feel a sharp pain as she half-missed the seat and hit the floor. She swore under her breath. "Sorry, Felice, I'll get you the dollar after school," she said. She got up and sat down with more force than necessary. A few people at a nearby table looked over and snickered.

Marlon pulled out his wallet and handed a dollar to his sister. "You OK, Abs? You don't feel dizzy or anything? If you need to go home or something..."

"I'm fine, Mars-Bars." She started eating her lunch, mind mulling over what just happened. No, she wasn't dizzy. Her head hurt a little. That was all. *Well, my head and my rear.*

Felice rolled her eyes and handed the bill back to her brother. "Just don't push yourself, Abs. I know you think you need perfect grades for college, but your health matters, too." She stabbed at her spaghetti with her fork.

"I know," Abby replied. She ate slowly, hoping the conversation would continue without her. Eventually her friends got the hint and left her to her thoughts. She turned to her guardians. *I'm overthinking this right? I just... missed the chair. Nothing more.* The bell rang well after she stopped anticipating their input, and she scrambled to dump her tray and get to her next class. *But Bjarte didn't take the credit and he would have... wouldn't he?*

For the first time since she'd started working for Sam, Abby was grateful for the dimness of the bar. It helped her headache, and the slower crowd during the week was much appreciated. She carried a tray of empty glasses back to the kitchen, humming along with the song on the jukebox.

"You know Sam wouldn't mind if you held off a few days."

I can't just let this derail my life, Dommy, she replied, smiling. She had noticed that Sam was keeping an eye on her. Halfway to the kitchen, she felt her shoelace catch under one foot. She stumbled before she could correct herself. The sound of shattering glass fought the sharp pain in her knees and hands for her attention. She looked at her shoes and found the left had come untied.

I tied them as tight as I could. I tucked the laces in... How did this happen? Never mind. Abby stood up and tied her shoe again, then turned around and came face to face with a broom-holding Sam. "Uh, thanks." She reached out for the broom.

Sam just turned around and started sweeping the mess up. "Maybe you ought to go lay down, Dragonfly. You only got off bed-rest a couple days ago."

"I..." Abby wanted to argue, but didn't want to be rude. "If I feel like I need to quit, I will, I promise. I tripped on my shoelaces, that's all."

"You better." He walked off with the dustpan full of glass. "Don't need the wasps coming down on my head."

Dominic shook his head. "Don't know why he can't just say he cares about you. Then again, he always was a gruff old coot."

Abby eyed her shoes, then went to check her tables. *I did just trip...*

right? Had to have. I'd have heard about it if... She narrowed her eyes and tried something. *If Screwtape had anything to do with it.* Nothing. No response at all. *OK, then.* After Bjarte's mocking reply to her scolding him over her boyfriend's name, Abby had expected his commentary to become far more frequent. Instead, he'd gone completely silent. *Am I the only one worried about that?*

"No," came her guardians' reply in unison.

"Whenever he ceases to be seen and heard," said Aeneas, "surely he is up to something."

"And I'd bet whatever it is," said Nick, "we won't like it at all."

"How did you even get up here?" Marlon asked Isaac as he struggled to reach the branch the boy was on. He'd had to get the ladder just to get halfway to him.

"Funny girl no one sees showed me." Isaac sat on the large branch like he was back in their room in the beanbag chair. "View up here's awesome!"

"One nobody see —" He pulled his foot up when a branch snapped under his weight. It fell a few feet before getting tangled. *Mom's not gonna be happy about that.* "Since when do you have an imaginary friend?"

"Don't," said Isaac. "She's real. She says you need to take that branch. It's stronger." He pointed to the thick one near Marlon's foot.

"Oh... kay." Marlon nervously did as he was told and found the branch could support him. After a few more tense moments, he finally laid a hand beside his brother. "Come on, Ike, let's get you down from here." His shivered nervously. *This reeks of Mr. Creepy's stunt with Abs...*

Isaac looked at him blankly. "Down? I dun wanna come down."

"It's almost dinner time, Isaac. If you don't come down Mom and Dad'll be mad." Marlon tried to quickly get his arm around his younger brother. "Come on."

Isaac scooted further along the branch, sticking out his tongue. Then he got a mischievous smile on his face. "OK, I'll get down." The boy backed off the branch and proceeded to swing from branch to branch until he reached the ladder. He scampered down and knocked the ladder over, leaving his would-be-savior stranded in the tree. He waved. "Buh-bye, Marlon!" He turned and disappeared into the house.

"Crap." Marlon kicked his legs in frustration as he tried to think of a way down that wouldn't end with broken bones. He already expected to be laughed at by his siblings until the end of time. Finally, he patted his pocket and pulled out his cell phone. "I just hope Abs ain't too busy."

Abby had just finished putting a TV dinner in the microwave when her phone rang. With a sigh, she walked over and answered it. "Yes, Marlon? Sam call your dad again?"

"About what?" His voice sounded strained. "Actually... Um. I've... kinda pulled a Dommy."

"You've given unnecessary commentary on my life choices?" Abby smirked at The Dragon lounging on her bed.

Dominic rolled his eyes. "You wouldn't have me any other way and you know it."

"Wrong Dommy. Abs... I'm stuck up a tree."

She went completely silent. "Marlon... are you serious?"

"Unfortunately."

"How did you even get...?"

"Three guesses and the first two don't count."

"Isaac. And you're calling me instead of your parents because...?"

"Because I'd rather I didn't have to hear about this until we're out of college. Could you come over, please? I just need the ladder back."

"You realize me showing up will draw attention to this anyway, right?" Abby turned off the microwave and got her car keys. "Unless you have a plan that will somehow get me past your parents." She shook her head at his instructions, then promised to be there as soon as she could safely. After she hung up, she laughed. "Now who's the white knight?"

"It's not that funny," said Dominic, taking his place at her heels. He   grinned   anyway.

CHAPTER 36

"Ah-bee!" Isaac ran to meet her when his mother let her in. "Marlon is –"

"Hey there, Isaac!" she said cheerfully, kneeling down and hugging the boy. "How about you show me where he is, hmm?"

"OK!" The boy took her hand and practically dragged her through the house and out the back door. He let go of her hand as he jumped off the step and raced over to the shade tree. "Up dere, Ah-bee! See?"

"Hey, Abs." Marlon sat on a branch, his feet propped on one below him, one hand holding his head and the other across his knees. "Fancy meeting you here."

She shook her head. "Mars-Bars, I swear." She looked around, found the ladder, and put it back against the tree. "What would you do without me?"

"Go insane?" he replied. He started to get up then jerked back against the branch. "Shoot!"

"What's wrong?" Abby gently pushed the laughing Isaac back toward the house. "Isaac, can you go and get me a pinecone? Thanks."

"Got my shirt caught," Marlon groaned. "Hold on."

"Why don't you go up and join him? Now that the unusually articulate brat's gone, that'd be a decently private place for a make-out session. Marlon and Abby, sittin' in a tree..."

182

"Quit stealing my lines, deceiver." Dominic growled softly. "Though, should have known you wouldn't be gone too long."

Abby debated, then said aloud, "I didn't know you even knew the word 'articulate', Bjarte. I'm honestly surprised. I always assumed Isaac had a better vocabulary."

"Bj –" Marlon's head jerked up, then she heard fabric rip as he pulled free and all but bolted down the ladder. "You start talkin' crap about my little brother and I'll –"

"Why you talking to the bad man?" Isaac returned, holding up a pinecone to Abby. "Don't you know you not supposed to talk to 'em?"

Abby took the pinecone wordlessly. "Isaac... you can see him? Hear him?"

Isaac looked genuinely confused. "Uh-huh." To her complete shock, he looked straight at The Dragon beside her. "Didn't you tell her not to talk to him? The funny lady told me that a long time ago. Don't talk to the bad people, then they can't hurt you."

"Thanks for the tip, Ike," said Marlon. He looked at Abby sideways before he put the ladder away. "Come on, let's get inside before we freeze, OK?"

Abby reached out and took Marlon's hand, lacing their fingers together as they went into the house. *How did he... how could he?* She couldn't wrap her head around someone else talking directly to Dominic.

"He is still innocent," said Aeneas. "His eyes are still unclouded by age and experience."

Isaac burst out giggling. "You don't know me too well do you, mister?"

Marlon's eyes shot to her face. "Do I even want to know?"

"Aeneas said Isaac can tell they're there because he's innocent."

"Yeah, right," said Marlon with a snort. "That'll be the day." He looked thoughtful for a moment, then asked, "Hey, why did you think Sam called Dad?"

"I tripped over my shoelaces and broke a bunch of glasses."

"Seriously, Abs. Next you'll think he'll be calling 'cause ya got a hangnail."

Abby shook her head. "The way he acts sometimes, I wouldn't be surprised."

Abby sighed. The warm shower relaxed both her body and mind. She hummed as she washed her hair, preparing for bed. She chuckled as she replayed Marlon's rescue that day. She turned around to get the washcloth and came face to face with a smirking Bjarte. She tried to back away in the confined space, but slipped on the shower floor and fell. Pain shot up her side and her already-abused head pounded from the jolt. She was unable to move, water pouring down her naked body and face.

"What the Hell just happened?" came Dominic's voice from the other side of the shower door. "Are you OK?"

"You don't really think you can just pretend I'm not here, do you?" he asked, his voice like velvet steel. "That ship sailed a long time ago."

Don't react, just move, she told herself, fighting the pain. With the water in her face, she couldn't open her eyes. Couldn't see him, but could sense him. *Don't respond.*

"It don't work," he said. "Your eyes done been open too long. You can't shut them now." He laughed. "Well, maybe you literally can, but ya know what I mean."

"ABIGAIL!"

"I'm fine," she replied. *Don't react, don't respond.* The pain dulled enough for her to stand. She felt her way back to her feet, found her washcloth and wiped her eyes. *Don't react.*

"Oh, OK, you want to play that game? Fine. I'll play."

Abby froze as she felt a hand in her hair, which slowly moved down her back. She jerked away before it could go lower, spinning around to glare at him. "You perverted slime ball!"

The demon just laughed. "Told ya so," he said, and vanished from sight.

CHAPTER 37

The rest of November dragged on, only broken up by the holiday visit to her grandmother, homework, and trying to figure out what to do about her grandfather's game.

"You're wasting your time." Bjarte's scorn was clear in his voice. "You're never going to get anyone interested in that relic."

And the deceiver's unwanted commentary. Abby sought refuge in rejoining the RP with her friends. They had been right. The founder proved to be a much saner admin. She was actually enjoying the game again, which almost allowed her to ignore him.

"Oooh, we're gonna play this again. OK, I'll start!"

"Don't. Touch. Me." Abby clenched her teeth as she worked on her homework. "Don't you have anything better to do?"

"I still stand by the succubus suggestion," said Dominic, growling. "Keep your hands to yourself, deceiver."

"Oh, come on." Bjarte laughed. "Seriously, it's the way things oughtta be. Girl your age shouldda already popped the cherry... but you're waiting for a wasp."

"Go to Hell." She finished off the last assignment and started tucking her books and papers back into her backpack.

"We already went over this. Been there, loved it. You'll like it, too."

"Too bad I'll never see it to find out." She tossed the backpack down beside her desk. "Now, go away." She logged on to the forum to check for replies, only to be disappointed. "Dang it." The messenger dinged and she smiled.

WaterHorse: OK, Dragonfly, I'll bite. What's this game Random keeps going on about you're trying to get out?

DragonflyGirl: "Path of the Dragon"? It's a video game my grandfather made. You play as a young boy in a world where people randomly become monsters, trying to save his brother who has become a dragon. It holds the record for being the only game Random couldn't beat.

WaterHorse: Oh really? *mischievous grin* You got a beta version? I like a challenge.

"Never thought about getting some of our game friends to try it." Abby tapped her fingers on the desk, then looked at Dominic. "What do you think?"

"Worth a shot," he replied from his place at her feet. "I'm not that concerned with it making money. I ain't that delusional. Word of mouth is gold in any business."

DragonflyGirl: You'd have to ask Random, computer stuff isn't my strong suit. If you do play it, I wanna hear your take on it. Considering I had the pleasure of watching Random throw a fit seven ways from Sunday.

WaterHorse: You got it. Now I've got to try this. See ya on the forum, Ava.

"See ya," she replied, grinning. "Well, that's a start."

"You sure your buddies won't just steal it and make the changes you won't?"

Abby bit her cheek to keep from snapping at him. She refreshed the forum for something to do. Anything but "talking to the bad people." Still nothing. The messenger dinged again.

RandomWord: You sure you're OK with WH having a copy of POTD?

DragonflyGirl: She's as game-crazy as you. Maybe we need to start building the fanbase. I'm sure Grandpa Nick wouldn't care if it became a free game with a ... what's the word?

RandomWord: Turning it into a cult classic might be a good idea. OK, I'll send her the file I've got. Cross your fingers.

RandomWord: So how ya doing, Abs?

DragonflyGirl: I'm OK for the most part. Isaac was onto something. You-Know-Who really doesn't care for the silent treatment.

RandomWord: Is that a good thing? I mean...

Abby debated what to say. The idea of telling Marlon that the deceiver was getting touchy-feely whenever she ignored him didn't sound like a great plan. But on the other hand, keeping secrets wasn't either. "If he had a physical form," she typed, "you'd have punched him by now. He's gone the dirty old man route to force a response."

RandomWord: The only words that come to mind would cost me a week's pay. I got your back, Abs. You need me, don't hesitate. I tipped the scales once. I can dang well do it again.

DragonflyGirl: If anything goes down, I'll contact you, promise. Just... keep praying. *sighs* Apparently it's more help than we thought.

RandomWord: Not a problem. The Man Upstairs and I seem to have an understanding, I guess. With everything handled... maybe I need to go back to Mass with you?

"Attending ceremonies covered in extravagant trappings has little to do with faith," Aeneas chimed in. "His acceptance that his requests are heard and considered is what matters."

She typed that to Marlon, then leaned back in her chair, confused. "So... wait. Does that mean I don't have to go to Mass either?"

"No shit Sherlock," said Bjarte. "You just gotta be 'good' and 'honor the Creator' and you can do whatever you want."

"It is not that simple and you know it," Aeneas snapped. "But he speaks this much truth. You do not have to attend any service. Though, in your case, it keeps you close to your path."

"I'm having the weirdest conversation right now," she typed to Marlon. She went on to explain what her guardian had said. "I don't get it. You can skip it, but it helps me?"

RandomWord: Every time I see you come out of Mass, you look so relaxed and happy. Refreshed. I dunno, it just seems to recharge your batteries. You never looked like that after Davidson's sermons. I should have taken before and after pictures.

Abby sat there, thinking that over. It was true. Mass did something for her that nothing else did. There, she felt close to God, safe, and loved. That was why her childhood church had been her chosen battleground when she'd suspected the presence behind her "imaginary friend".

RandomWord: It's like... to me it's like you don't defend yourself with martial arts if you're better with a sword unless you have no choice. Mass... your faith... that's your sword, Abs. You just need to keep it sharp.

She smiled. "It's no wonder the enemy doesn't want you around, Mars-Bars," she replied. "I can't imagine anyone I'd rather have on my side."

RandomWord: Back at ya Abs. Love you.

DragonflyGirl: Love you, too.

CHAPTER 38

Abby drove slowly through the recently plowed roads, two bouquets in the passenger seat beside her. She risked a glance in her rear view mirror at the unusually silent dragon lounging in the back seat. Only trips like this could stem his commentary. Once she had gotten her driver's license, she had made one major change to her holiday routine, one she had not dared bring up to Gladys. Soon enough, the car bounced along the snow-dusted gravel roads of the cemetery until she reached her parents' graves.

Abby reached for the bouquets and stepped out of the car. She walked over to the headstones and lay each one down. The stones weren't fancy. Simple gray rock carved with names and dates that meant little to anyone but her. *Almost no one.* She smiled at the fresh boot prints that weren't hers. A small bundle of daisies, pink carnations, and violets wrapped in a black ribbon had already been laid upon the graves. The sight never failed to put a lump in her throat, as she recognized where they came from. Small pots of each flower decorated the Samsons' living room, grown by Marlon's mother.

"Hi, Mom, Daddy," she said softly. "A lot's happened since I was last here. I'm sorry I can't stay long. I've got to get to Grandma's before Mars-Bars freaks out and thinks I wrecked or something." She took her gloved hand and knocked the snow off the stones, then traced the names. "Did you send Domino, by the way? If you did, thanks. Give True a scratch behind the ears for me, OK? And tell him he's not been replaced. He's still my cuddle buddy."

"You better be takin' care of my girl, Cowboy," said Dominic, coming to sit beside her. "I'm takin' care of yours, don't worry." He folded his ears as one paw brushed his daughter's stone. "Don't let the boy drive St. Pete too crazy, Nicky, OK? I want you two to be there when I get there." The Dragon sighed. "I will get there, and so will your girl."

"I love you," Abby whispered, brushing her fingers across the stones one last time before turning back to the car. "We'll be back." She waited until The Dragon got in the car, then slid into the driver's seat and headed for her grandmother's.

"You all are simply incorrigible," said Gail as they finished their off-key rendition of "We Wish You a Merry Christmas." She shook her head. "I told you I'd be fine." She picked up the boxes from under the tree and started handing them out.

"You said the same thing last year, dear, and the year before," Vera calmly reminded her, passing a box on to her daughter-in-law. "What made you think they would listen this time?"

"Respect for their elders, maybe?" Gail laughed. "I'm pretty sure we're breaking a maximum capacity rule here."

Abby smiled as she looked around at her grandmother's living room, packed to the brim with what Sam kept calling her "future in-laws." Ever since reacquainting themselves, Bryan and Vera had made a point to visit Gail and get her out of the apartment as much as possible. They also made sure that Abby wasn't the only one who kept Gail company for Christmas, countering the widow's protests that they should spend time with their own family by dragging the whole clan along.

"Even if they were breaking all the rules, pretty sure Wasp wouldn't care." Dominic smirked as he watched his friend sneak behind Vera. "He's a bit too reckless for his own good."

What makes you say that? Abby burst out laughing as Bryan calmly held some mistletoe over his wife's head, placed a quick kiss on the cheek, then bolted toward the door.

"NOT IN PUBLIC!" The elder Mrs. Samson's face turned scarlet as she took off after her husband. "Bumbler, I swear! You never learn!"

"Of course I learn," Bryan countered with a grin. "Why ya think I'm runnin'?" Unfortunately his escape was cut short by a casually outstretched leg and he tumbled to the floor. Bryan glared up at the offender. "Thanks a lot, Firecracker."

"Anytime, Dad."

Vera grabbed Bryan's collar and proceeded to drag him into the kitchen. "I'd deal with this here, but I think the children value their eyesight."

Abby laughed at the chorus of protests that rang out, at least until a pair of arms wrapped around her and a pair of lips brushed her cheek. She flushed. "MARS-BARS!"

He laughed and stood up. Then he reached into his jacket pocket. He knelt in front of Abby on one knee and held out a ring box. "This time... I am asking. Will you marry me?"

The whole room held its breath, waiting for her answer.

THAT'S ALL FOR NOW, BUT HERE'S A SNEAK PEAK AT THE SEQUEL

Headlights pushed through the curtains and chased each other across the floor as cars passed by Abby's window. The streetlights kept the room from the sheltering darkness she craved. Music drifted through floor from the bar below.

Tears rolled unchecked down her face. Abby hugged her pillow to her chest. She sat on the edge of her bed, rocking back and forth. I can't do this. This can't be happening. I'm not strong enough... She looked down at the bracelet on her wrist. Its charms reflected the light, bright even in the dim room. *If I was less jaded I'd say they're like hope or something. But they're not.* She closed her eyes. *They are just bits of metal and plastic.* She felt her cat nudge against her side, his concern clear in his meows.

"Abigail." Dominic's voice was concerned but firm. "You are strong enough for this. You are wiser than you know, and braver too."

"I don't feel strong." Abby let go of the pillow to cradle her cat. Even Domino's purring wasn't enough to lift her spirits. "I feel like I'm about to shatter into a million pieces."

"If you do, you will come together again." Aeneas sat down beside her, leaving her other side to his former charge. "You will heal, Abigail, I know you are strong enough to do so."

"I wish I had your confidence." Abby reached a hand to her neck and rubbed her cross between her thumb and fore-finger. "I'm not the Dragon. I'm just the dragonfly."

"You know." Dominic brushed his paw against the dragonfly charm on her bracelet. "A legend I heard long ago that says dragonfly was once dragon. That it became such when it was challenged to prove its power... By Coyote, I think."

Abby looked at him in confusion. "Why did the dragon turn into a dragonfly?"

"In accepting the challenge to prove its power, it lost the power."

"Great, just great." Abby glared at the floor. "So what does that make me? The dragon that failed?"

"I didn't say that." Dominic examined the charm again. "To me, a dragonfly is simply a dragon that rose to the challenge."

ABOUT THE AUTHOR

Ashleigh Daniellé Jaelyn Cutler is the daughter of two avid readers. She had a book in her hand before she could walk. One of her favorite phrases, when she began to talk, quickly became "Daddy book read". Her parents, Jay Cutler and Pam Stepp, offered constant encouragement and praise as she made her way towards becoming the artist and author she always wanted to be.

Her stories, supported by the various courses she took during her school years, explore a range of social topics despite their often non-human protagonists. Her artwork does focus more on wolves at times as well as the stars of these tales. Also known online as Ash Of Wolves until 2004, she adopted the handle AshWolf Forever in 2009 and still uses it today. She can be found on Facebook, Twitter, deviantART.com, GoodReads.com. Fanfiction.net and FictionPress.com.

She is currently working on her next book.

OTHER TITLES BY ASHLEIGH D.J. CUTLER
A Childhood Fantasy
Few Know You're Crying
Mask of the Dragon
and many more to come, including *Heir of the Dragon*.

www.ingramcontent.com/pod-product-compliance
Lightning Source LLC
Chambersburg PA
CBHW071511170626
46811CB00007B/2812